Murder, M

MW00423417

Leighann Dobbs

This is a work of fiction. None of it is real.

All names, places, and events are products of the author's imagination. Any resemblance to real names, places, or events are purely coincidental, and should not be construed as being real.

Chapter One

"She said the marzipan was *atrocious*!" Lexy looked down at the miniature fruits she had carefully sculpted the day before with the help of her assistant, Cassie. The tiny candies were made from her own almond paste recipe and had been carefully shaped, painted, and sugared to look like miniature versions of actual fruit. She thought they had come out perfectly.

Cassie wrinkled her forehead. Popping a tiny pear into her mouth, she chewed enthusiastically. "Tastes great to me. *Sergeant* Saunders is just mean and I'll tell you, she doesn't seem to like us at all."

Lexi nodded in agreement. Amanda Scott-Saunders had been a judge at the national bakers competition, *Bakery Battle*s, for the past ten years. She was known for her harsh criticisms and nasty remarks. She had brought contestants to tears more than once, much to the delight of the sponsors who claimed it was good for ratings.

Lexy thought it fitting that everyone called her "Sergeant Saunders" behind her back. The woman had all the sensitivity and finesse of a drill sergeant and delighted in crushing the hopes of contestants. She had taken a particular dislike to Lexy. No matter how pleased the other judges were with Lexy's work, Saunders always found something to complain about. It was a miracle Lexy was tied for first place in the competition.

"She said if I kept producing food like the marzipan, I would be out of the competition." Lexy felt her face flush with anger. "If you ask me, the competition would be much better off if *she* was out of it."

Lexy heard a giggle from the booth next to hers. She swung her head towards the sound. Her eyes locked on the ice-blue gaze of Aurea Pearce, her closest competition with whom she was currently tied for first place.

"I guess the Sergeant didn't like your little fruits," she said in a sickly-sweet voice. Lexy noticed her lips were curled in a smile that didn't reach her hard, cold eyes.

Lexy wasn't fooled by the sweet, Barbie doll appearance of the petite blonde. Aurea was the type that acted nice to your face, but stabbed you in the back as soon as you turned around. She was a ruthless competitor who would stop at nothing to win.

Lexy plastered a smile on her face. "You win some, you lose some," she said matter-of-factly as if the dressing down she received the afternoon before didn't faze her in the least. She'd be damned if she'd let Aurea Pearce know it bothered her; the other woman would probably find some way to use it against her.

Lexy turned back to Cassie. "I'm going to put these in the community freezer." She held up the tray of marzipan.

Cassie nodded, her head bent over a three-tiered wedding cake that was the subject of the days competition. Lexy smiled at the contrast of Cassie's pink spiked hair against the traditional white roses she was applying to the cake.

Lexy took a deep breath. The sting of the previous days judging still hurt, but today was another day and she was determined not to let the harsh words of Amanda Scott-Saunders throw her off course and ruin her chances of realizing her childhood dream.

Lexy looked around the giant stadium hall that housed the set of *Bakery Battles*, a yearly competition of the best bakers in America. The space consisted of dozens of kitchen areas, one for each baker. She was honored to be chosen and thrilled she had already made it through several rounds. She considered it one of the greatest accomplishments of her culinary career. The exposure for her bakery *The Cup and Cake* plus the chance of winning a $100,000 prize and a spread in *American Baker Magazine* didn't hurt either.

With renewed vigor for the days competition, she hurried off to the giant community freezer to store the marzipan, the echo of her Christian Loboutin stilettos tapping on the concrete as she made her way across the vast stadium.

Lexy reached out for the smooth handle of the freezer, the tray of marzipan balanced in one hand. The door opened easily, welcoming Lexy in a blanket of icy air.

She felt herself shiver. *They must have the thermostat turned way down today.* Not wanting to spend too much time in the arctic environment, she hurried down the aisle to her designated storage spot. Her heel caught on one of the open holes of the thick rubber mat. Jerking forward, she caught herself from falling but not before a dozen assorted marzipan fruits fell to the floor.

"Damn it!"

Lexy put the tray on the shelf and bent down to retrieve the marzipan. With a surge of annoyance, she noticed a few pieces had bounced under the metal shelving. She almost had to lie on the floor to reach under the shelf to get them.

Her apron dragged through the dirt on the mat. She made a mental note to pick up a new one from the hangers in the back of the freezer.

Stretching her arm under the shelf she felt blindly for the fruit. Her hand encountered something squishy...and big.

"What the heck..."

Lexy put her face down at floor level to peer under the shelf. She felt a jolt run through her body. Her lungs burned, filling with a deep breath of icy-cold air. Her mouth opened to yell, but nothing came out. Her eyes blinked closed as if to erase what she was seeing. Fear squeezed her heart when she opened them again and realized the scene was still the same.

She was staring into the cold, dead eyes of Amanda Scott-Saunders.

Chapter Two

"Why were you in the freezer?"

"I was dropping off some marzipan...to freeze for later." Lexy squinted up at the police detective. Feeling a bit light headed, she rubbed her temples.

"Are you all right, ma'am?"

"Yes." Lexy shook herself. "It's just that I don't find bodies every day. It's a bit disturbing."

The detective- Detective Ryan, it said on his badge- put a gentle hand on her shoulder. "You sit here and relax. Detective Stone will have more questions for you."

"Detective Stone?"

"The detective in charge. Nik will be here shortly, until then just sit tight...and don't leave the area."

Detective Nik Stone. The name made her think wistfully of her boyfriend back home, Detective Jack Perillo. They had actually met under similar circumstances: Lexy's ex-boyfriend had been poisoned with cupcakes from her bakery and Jack had been the detective in charge. Hopefully Nik Stone would be as easy to work with, and hopefully she could get things to go in her favor with a few well-placed flirtations, just like she had done with Jack.

Lexy heard a commotion to her right. The place was crawling with police who all seemed to stop and look in the direction of the commotion. Suddenly the detective was back at her side.

"This is the woman who found the body. Lexy Baker - Detective Stone."

Lexy stuck out her hand, then felt her eyes grow wide. Her mouth dropped open as she stared at the head detective. Tall. Commanding. Exuding as much authority as any man Lexy had ever met.

Except Nik Stone wasn't a man. Detective Nik Stone was one of the most beautiful women Lexy had even seen. *So much for getting things to go my way by batting my eyelashes.*

Nik grabbed Lexy's outstretched hand. Even though her hands were delicate and perfectly manicured, her handshake was firm and strong - not a girly handshake at all. Lexy watched the detective pull up a chair opposite her. Her no-nonsense black flats planted on the floor seemed to accentuate her long, thin legs. Lexy noticed her willowy frame had been well equipped in the chest department. Lexy felt a pang of jealousy; the woman had the body of a showgirl.

Detective Stone leaned forward, her copper-red hair billowing around her alabaster skin like a cloud. She fixed Lexy with a commanding stare, her golden orbs drilling into Lexy's green ones.

"OK, Ms. Baker, why don't you tell me what you were doing here and how you found the body."

Lexy recited the story of her tripping on the mat, then finding the body under the shelf in an attempt to retrieve the marzipan.

"I see. So you are in the competition?"

Lexy nodded.

"And what is your relationship to the judge?"

Lexy bit her bottom lip. "None. I mean, only that she's a judge here. I didn't know her before or anything."

"She judged your baking?" Nik fired off the questions rapidly, giving Lexy little time to think.

"Yes."

"Favorably?"

Lexy felt a nervous tic start in her eye. "Well, not really. I mean, she was *supposed* to be critical of them."

Nik nodded, then leaned even closer. "So, you might say you had an adversarial relationship with the victim?"

Lexy felt her shoulders start to tense up. "Well, not just me...pretty much everyone here did."

She glanced around. The activity in *Bakery Battles Stadium* had come to a halt. Most of the bakers and their assistants were standing around, trying to get a good view.

She saw Cassie push her way through the crowd, elbowing people aside to get to Lexy.

"What's going on?" Cassie looked from Lexy to Nik.

Lexy took a deep breath and lifted her chin toward the freezer. "I found another body."

"*Another* body?" Nik arched a perfectly plucked brow.

Lexy felt her cheeks grow warm. She stabbed her index finger into her eye to stop her spastically twitching eyelid. "I found one before... not here...on a catering job back home," she stammered.

Nik stared at her incredulously. "So, you make it a habit to stumble over dead bodies. That sounds a bit suspicious to me."

"I don't kill them, I just happen to be the one who finds them." Lexy shrugged, then breathed a sigh of relief when the other detective - the nice one - returned, commanding Nik's attention.

"The M.E. is almost done with the body. Did you want to look at it?"

Nik stood. "Yes, what was the TOD?"

"She said it's hard to tell since the body was frozen but her guess is around 4 am."

"Cause of death?"

"Strangled...with something very thin. We haven't found it yet though."

Nik nodded. "Have Styles and McManus interview everyone else in the stadium. Don't let anyone leave until they've talked to them. And get the crew looking for what she was strangled with."

Nik turned to Lexy. "You can go now, but don't leave the city. I'm going to want to talk to you lat-"

A commotion over by the freezer door stole Nik's attention. A third detective appeared in the doorway holding something up in his latex-gloved hands. "Found the murder weapon."

Lexy felt her heart clench. He was holding one of the aprons the competition doled out to every contestant. The aprons were all the same, except each was embroidered with the contestants initials. The one he held up had the initials "LB".

Amanda Scott-Saunders had been strangled with one of Lexy's aprons.

Chapter Three

"I thought she was going to lock you up on the spot!" Cassie looked at Lexy wide-eyed.

Lexy nodded in agreement. Detective Nik Stone had seemed quite suspicious of her, especially after the apron was found, but Lexy knew Stone would need more than that to arrest her.

"I can't say I'm sorry she's dead," Lexy admitted. "But I don't like the way some of the evidence points at me."

"Well, at least now we might have a better chance of winning the contest," Cassie pointed out.

Lexy glanced over at the next booth. Aurea was huddled in the corner whispering with Grace Harvey, one of the alternate judges. Lexy felt her stomach drop as she realized someone would have to replace Saunders. If that someone was Grace Harvey, things might be even worse for her.

There wasn't much she could do about it at the moment, so she turned her attention to more pressing matters.

"The filming is canceled for today, but I think we should still work on the cakes so they will be perfect for judging tomorrow."

Cassie nodded her agreement, then went straight to the fridge at the back of the makeshift kitchen and pulled out several cake tiers. The next part of the contest would judge them on their cake-decorating skills as well as on the complexity and taste of the cakes.

Lexy had planned to "wow" the judges with a traditional white three-tier cake decorated to the nines with a quilted-texture fondant covered in white frosting roses and silver leaves and balls. The cake itself was vanilla and she was adding in raspberry liqueur filling to give it some extra punch.

The grooms cake was a funky contemporary design with geometric tiers offset and covered in bright, colors and decorations. The frosting was all smooth fondant cut out into interesting shapes. Chocolate fudge cake with toffee caramel filling would please the palates while the decoration of the cake would please the judges eyes. Or at least that's what Lexy hoped.

The mornings events, however, had somewhat dampened her enthusiasm for cake decorating. *Would she even be around to present the cakes or would she be sitting in jail...or worse: disqualified from the competition?*

Lexy looked around the stadium. Each row was sectioned off with fabric in the back so she couldn't see the entire room. From her kitchen she could see the other kitchens in the same row as well as the ones across from her. Glancing around, she noticed most of the bakers were focusing on getting their cakes made, but some were looking over at her suspiciously. *Did they all think she had done it?*

Lexy went over to the fridge and pulled out a bowl of golden caramel that had been setting up in preparation for its role in the grooms cake. She grabbed some toffee from her supply rack and started crushing it with a rolling pin, adding it in small amounts to the caramel.

"We need to do something to help catch the killer soon so I can put my energies into the contest and not have to worry about when Detective Stone is going to appear with a pair of handcuffs in my size."

Cassie nodded. "We're both up to our eyeballs here with work, but maybe tonight we can set aside some time to talk to some of the other bakers and see if we can find anything out."

Lexy popped a piece of toffee into her mouth, rolling it around on her tongue. She moved it from side to side savoring the buttery taste while she brushed the rest of the toffee into the bowl and covered it with plastic wrap.

"Yeah, it's too bad we are so limited on time..." Lexy's head jerked up. "Wait a minute, *we* don't have a lot of time, but I know someone who does and she's the perfect person to help us find the killer."

Cassie arched her brows. "You don't mean..."

"Yes, I do." Lexy whipped off her apron and threw it on the shelf. "You stay here and mind the fort, I think I know just where to find her."

Lexy stood in the wide entrance to the casino. The clamor of bells and blinking lights caused a momentary disorientation. She scanned the rows of slot machines looking for her grandmother's familiar bluish-gray head.

She spotted her on the other side of the casino. Mona Baker, or Nans, as Lexy had called her since childhood, sat at her favorite "Wheel of Fortune" slot machine happily pressing buttons. Lexi smiled at the flushed look of excitement on the woman's face.

When Lexi had made the reservations for her Las Vegas trip to compete in *Bakery Battles*, she had invited Nans along, knowing how much the older woman loved playing the slots. She figured since she had rented two rooms for her and Cassie anyway, it would be an inexpensive way for Nans to have a vacation. Little did she know she would have to avail herself of the older woman's detective skills to help solve a murder.

Lexy aimed for Nans, navigating the sea of gamblers. She passed a little bar inside the casino. Someone inside the bar caught her eye. She slowed down for a better look.

Was that...?

It was! Amanda Scott-Saunders's husband sat at the corner of the bar. Normally, the man was meticulously groomed; Lexy felt a pang of sympathy as she noticed his rumpled shirt, tired eyes and stubbled chin. Sympathy soon turned to suspicion, however, when she saw that one hand held a tall drink and the other was draped around the back of a chair that held a striking blonde. Her eyes narrowed as she watched them talking and laughing.

Hours after his wife was found murdered? She mentally added Peter Saunders to her suspect list, then continued to navigate her way over to the bank of blinking slot machines where Nans was seated.

"Are you winning?" Lexy asked as she approached the older woman.

Nans swiveled her head in Lexy's direction only long enough to indicate she heard her, then returned to watching the reels spin.

"Not so much, about even," Nans said holding her hand out flat and tilting it back and forth.

"Did you hear?" Lexy asked.

"Hear what?" This time Nans didn't even turn her head.

"There was a murder this morning in Bakery Battles Stadium."

That got her attention. Nans turned to face Lexy, the slot machine all but forgotten. "Really?"

Lexy told her about how she had discovered the body, the police inquisition and the discovery of her apron as the murder weapon.

"That nasty woman." Nans looked like she'd eaten a sour lemon. "There's probably a lot of people who would have wanted to kill her."

"Only every baker in the competition. I also noticed her husband is in the bar over there," Lexy tilted her head in the direction of the bar, "living it up with some blonde."

Nans' eyes widened. She craned her neck to get a view of the bar.

"And I noticed Aurea Pearce is very friendly with Grace Harvey. If Grace replaces Amanda it could throw the competition in Aurea's favor."

"Do you think she would stoop to murder just to win the competition? I know there is a lot of money at stake, but murder?"

Lexy worried her bottom lip with her teeth. *Did she think Aurea would stoop to murder?*

"It does seem a bit extreme, but no harm in checking her out, right?" Lexy shrugged. "Nans, I was hoping you and the ladies would help look into some of the suspects. Right now all the evidence points to me and I'm so busy with the competition..."

"Of course, dear." She slid off her seat, grabbing her gigantic purse. "I'll go back to the room and call Ida.

Lexy felt relief wash over her. Earlier in the year she had discovered that her grandmother and her four friends had an odd hobby - they solved murders. In fact, they had been instrumental in finding the killer of Lexy's ex-boyfriend and in helping to clear her name from the suspect list. Their investigative skills had also come in handy when Lexy had stumbled across the dead body of a client several months earlier. Lexy felt a lot better knowing they were going to be helping to find Amanda's real killer and get the police off her back.

"Thanks, Nans. I knew I could count on you." Lexy noticed the older woman squinting at something just over her shoulder.

"Who is that?" Nans asked.

Lexy turned. She spotted the object of Nans' question about 20 feet away, making a beeline toward her. Detective Nik Stone.

Lexy's stomach rolled over as she watched the tall red-head barreling toward her, a trail of detectives in her wake.

"Your assistant told us we could find you here."

Lexy raised an eyebrow, afraid to speak. She noticed Nik looking at Nans. *She wouldn't arrest a girl in front of her grandmother, would she?*

"This is my grandmother, Mona Baker - Nans, this is Detective Nik Stone."

Lexy was surprised to see the stoic detective's face soften as she reached her hand out to Nans.

"Call me Nikki, Ms Baker."

Nik turned back to Lexy. "I need to ask you some questions. We've found out a few things that make you a person of interest in this case."

Lexy raised her eyebrows. "What?" she squeaked out.

"We reviewed the videos from yesterday. It seems Judge Saunders gave you quite a smack on your marzipan."

Lexy shrugged. "I already told you that this morning."

Nik flipped open her notebook thumbing through a few pages. "Yes, but what you didn't tell us is that afterward, you said the competition would be '*better if Saunders wasn't around*'." Nik wiggled her fingers in the air to punctuate the last five words.

Lexy swallowed. "That's just the sort of thing you say without really meaning anything. I was steaming about the bad judgment. I wouldn't actually kill her over it!"

"Your competitor Aurea Pearce seems to think you might."

Lexy felt her cheeks grow red with anger. *It would be just like Aurea to say that*. She took a deep breath. "Detective, Aurea Pearce is my biggest competition. She'll say pretty much anything to cast suspicion on me."

Nik nodded. "There is one more thing. We've done a little checking, and it seems this isn't the first time you've been suspected of murder."

"I already told you about my client..."

"Not that murder, your ex-boyfriend."

"But I was cleared. I was even the one who caught the real killer - with Nans' help." Lexy turned to her grandmother who nodded in agreement.

Nik raised an eyebrow at Nans. "Be that as it may, I have a call in to Detective Perillo back in Brooke Ridge Falls regarding you, so if you are hiding anything, you better come clean now. Jack and I are old friends."

Old friends? Lexy didn't like the predatory gleam in Nik Stone's eye when she said Jack's name. Nor did she like the fact that Jack hadn't mentioned he knew a gorgeous female detective out here. Then again, he probably wasn't expecting her to get involved in a murder case.

"I'm sure you'll find I'm not hiding anything." Lexy bristled.

"Well, then, I trust you won't leave the hotel. We may have more questions for you once we review the surveillance tapes and electronic room key records." She nodded at Nans. "A pleasure to meet you ma'am."

Nik turned in a billow of copper hair and strode off on her long legs, the detectives trailing behind her.

Lexy let out a breath she hadn't even realized she was holding. Jack was going to be mad when he found out she had gotten herself involved in another murder. He wasn't too happy when she'd investigated the last one and had made her promise she wouldn't get involved in any more.

"Well, I can see why you are in such a hurry to find the killer." Nans interrupted her thoughts.

"Exactly. Judge Saunders was nasty to everyone in the competition. That means we have a lot of suspects to weed through. I need to get busy finding out which one of them was *not* in their room at 4 am."

"I'll go back to the room and get the girls working on checking out Judge Saunders and Aurea Pearce. We can compare notes when you get up there."

"Thanks." Lexy bent over, giving Nans a quick hug before the women headed off in different directions.

Lexy exited the casino making a mental "to-do" list. She had to put some finishing touches on the wedding cakes for tomorrow's judging, then she wanted to talk to as many of the other

24

contestants as she could to see if they had noticed anything that could help her find the murderer.

Most importantly, she needed to figure out how to keep Jack from finding out she was investigating another murder. She had a gut feeling that keeping their relationship intact depended on preventing Detectives Perillo and Stone from talking to each other. Not only to keep Jack from finding out about her involvement in the case but also to keep the two of them from rekindling any old *friendship* they may have had.

Chapter Four

"It must have been scary finding her body." Corinne stared at Lexy wide-eyed.

"It gets your adrenalin going, that's for sure." Lexy looked around the other baker's booth which had wedding cake decorations neatly laid out. "Did you hear if they are going to be starting up the filming again tomorrow?"

Corinne nodded. "The show must go on."

Lexy studied the other woman. A perky girl in her mid-twenties, she was a good baker and a nice person. Lexy knew how much Corinne wanted to win *Bakery Battles* - her husband had left her with three kids and a mountain of debt. She desperately needed the money.

For a fleeting second, Lexy wondered if the death of Judge Saunders would help Corinne's chances. If Corinne thought it would, could she have murdered her?

Lexy shook off her suspicions. Was she getting so paranoid that she saw potential killers everywhere?

"Did you notice anything suspicious about Sanders or see anything that morning?"

Corinne shook her head. "I didn't get down here until six, and I heard she was killed much earlier. I was in my room all night with Kara."

Most of the contestants had roommates - other bakers they had teamed up with to share expenses. This made things a little easier for Lexy and her investigation since each baker had someone who could vouch for their whereabouts. Of course, that assumed they were all telling the truth.

The baker in the next booth, Mikela, leaned across the table separating the booths. "The police came by asking us all where we were and if anyone could confirm we were in our rooms. They said they could tell if anyone left because of the electronic room keys. The doors record when they are opened and closed. The only thing is, if the room door is opened, they don't know *who* left."

"To tell you the truth, I don't think anyone in the competition is too upset about Saunders, but I hate to think one of us killed her."

Lexy felt a chill at the young woman's words. The three woman looked around the stadium at the other bakers. *Could one of them be a cold-blooded killer?*

Mikela leaned in closer to Lexy and Corinne. "I didn't say too much to the police - none of us really want to because we're afraid of getting the competition closed down, but I did notice Judge Saunders was acting kind of funny."

Lexy felt her heart beat pick up speed. "Funny how?"

"She was acting kind of secretive - more so than usual. I saw her getting chummy in the corner with Evan Westmore a few times."

"Evan Westmore - the event coordinator?" Corinne made a sour face. "Who would want to get chummy with him?"

Lexy and Mikela chuckled. Westmore wasn't exactly handsome. He was actually rather dowdy - a short, stubby man with a bad attitude. Given Saunders's own nasty attitude, Lexy thought they might have made a perfect match.

"Hey, now that you mention it, I did notice she had some expensive new shoes and clothes. I didn't realize competition judges got paid so much."

"Did you see the Coach purse she had? I wondered why she seemed to be taking pains with her appearance. Maybe she was having an affair with Westmore?"

Lexy opened her mouth, pointed her finger at her throat, and made gagging noises causing the other two to collapse into a fit of giggles.

The laughter caught the attention of Janice, one of the other bakers, who came over to join them.

"We were just talking about Judge Saunders's murder," Corinne offered.

Janice raised an eyebrow. "Yeah, the police have been all over asking questions." She looked around the room, then stepped closer to the other women. "Some I'd rather not answer."

"Oh?" Lexy asked. "Like what?"

"They were asking us if we were in our rooms all night, if we had anyone in there, and what time we left."

"Right, they asked all of us."

"Well, I don't really like my roommate, but I don't want to be a tattle-tale either."

"Who is your roommate?"

"Aurea Pearce."

Lexy, Mikela and Corinne groaned in sympathy. No one liked Aurea, and to be saddled with her as a roommate seemed cruel.

"What do you know that you didn't want to tell them?" Lexy asked.

Janice looked down at the floor. "They asked me to verify what time Aurea and I left the room in the morning. Apparently she had told them she

29

left at 5 am. I told them I got up at 5:30 and left around 6 and that Aurea had left before me."

"That sounds about right., I don't see the problem." Corinne said wrinkling her brows together.

Janice bit her lower lip. "Aurea made a lot of noise when she got up and it woke me. I looked at the clock when she left and it wasn't 5 am like she said...it was 3:25 am - shortly before Saunders was murdered."

"How long until you can get all these surveillance tapes looked at?" Nik perched herself on the edge of Detective Jake Ryan's desk.

"Days, boss." He shrugged up at her. "The bakers' rooms are on all different floors and not all of them are staying in the hotel. It's gonna take a long time."

Nik chewed on an already stubby thumb-nail. They had questioned all the bakers in the competition and they were proving to be a tight lipped bunch.

"It's too bad they don't have cameras right in Bakery Battles Stadium. That would make our jobs a lot easier," Nik said wistfully.

"That's for sure. Unfortunately, the contestants wouldn't hear of it. They didn't want any cameras spying on their secret recipes."

Nik nodded. "Well, you know how I love a challenge. What do we have so far?"

Jake hit a few keys on the keyboard, then swung his monitor in her direction. "We have a dead bakery contest judge - TOD about 4 am. We have a bunch of contestants who hated her - they might all have had a motive. We've been able to verify that about half of them were in their rooms at the time of death so they can be ruled out. We have reports that the judge and her husband were fighting quite loudly the day before. That's about it."

"The husband...does he have an alibi?"

Jake shook his head. "He was in their room alone at the time of the murder. He did seem upset when we first informed him of his wife's death, but when I went back to question him later, he was in the casino drinking and didn't seem upset at all. He *did* say they were having troubles, but to tell you the truth he was so drunk it was hard to get anything concrete out of him. I have a note to go back and question him again."

"What about Lexy Baker, the one who found the body? Saunders was strangled with her apron.

Do you think she is involved?" Nik remembered the call she had put into Jack Perillo to check up on Baker. She pulled out her cell phone. No messages. *Same old Jack, gets so involved in his cases he forgets to look at his messages.*

"I'm not sure about her," Jake said. "She doesn't have much of a motive, even though the evidence points to her. Someone could be trying to frame her, or it could be co-incidence. Murder is pretty serious; most people don't kill someone over losing a contest...unless they have another reason."

Nik glanced at her watch. "We need to get more answers before the trail gets cold. It's too bad the contestants aren't more forthcoming with their information."

"They don't want to do anything to get the contest shut down. Maybe we should threaten them with pulling the plug on the whole thing unless they start coming forward with what they know,." Jake offered.

Nik screwed up one side of her face while she thought about it. It might work, but then again, it could also backfire on them. What they needed was a way to get them to open up...to gain some sort of an "in" with the bakers.

A sudden inspiration hit. She snapped her fingers. "I've got it!"

Jake raised his eyebrows for her to continue.

"The bakers won't talk to *us*, but they will talk to *each other*, especially Lexy Baker. What if we could get close to her and let her do the work for us?"

"What do you mean?"

"Make friends with her, maybe feed her some information. Let her get the dirt from the other bakers. I've seen her snooping around - if she's not the killer, then she might be able to lead us to whoever is."

Jake chewed the end of his pencil. "That might work, but how do we get chummy with her?"

Nik looked down at Jake. His straight white teeth worked the end of his pencil. His baby-blue eyes stared up at her from his handsome, finely chiseled face. A face that exuded honesty and trust but that was dotted with just enough stubble to give him a roguish air. *What woman could resist a face like that?*

"Not *we*, Detective Ryan - *you*."

Chapter Five

Lexy leaned back against the pillows, stretching her legs out on the bed. Her hand absently patted the spot beside her where her dog, Sprinkles, would be lying if she were at home.

She missed Sprinkles. The little white poodle mix was a big part of her life but Lexy couldn't bring her to Vegas so she had left the dog with Jack.

Jack!

She cringed, realizing he'd probably heard about the murder by now. She'd have to call him and downplay her role in it.

"...out anything interesting?" Nans' question interrupted her thoughts.

"What?" She looked over at the older woman sitting at the round table in their hotel room. Her iPad sat in front of her with the crossword puzzle and pencil next to it.

The room was a decent size with two queen beds. Lexy lay on the one nearest the table. She could see into the adjoining room through the open door. She and Cassie had rented two rooms so the three of them would have lots of space. In the next room, she could hear Cassie making showering noises which reminded her that she needed to hit the shower herself to wash off the days accumulation of flour and sugar.

"I asked if you had found out anything more downstairs - you were going to talk to the other bakers." Nans raised her eyebrows at Lexy.

"Oh, right. Actually I found out something very interesting. I talked to Aurea's roommate - she said Aurea wasn't in the room at the time Judge Saunders was murdered."

Nans' eyes went wide. "That *is* interesting. Would she have a motive to kill Saunders?"

"Her good friend Grace Harvey is one of the replacement judges. If Grace takes Saunders's spot, she might judge Aurea's work more favorably and give her a better chance of winning. There's a lot of money at stake."

Nans tapped her lips with her pencil. "Murdering someone is a pretty drastic move to win a contest, even if the prize is $100,000 and a magazine spread. I think the killer must have had a more pressing motive."

Nans' iPad erupted in a sequence of beeps and rings making Lexy jump. "What's that?"

"Oh, its FaceTime." Nans looked down at the tablet. "Ida's calling." She slid something on the screen, then peered down into it.

Ida's voice blared out of the tiny tablet. "Good evening Mona. How are things in Vegas?"

Lexy sat up on the bed leaning forward so she could see the iPad. The wide screen was filled with a closeup of her grandmother's friend and fellow amateur detective. The angle gave her face a somewhat distorted appearance magnifying her many wrinkles. Lexy stifled a giggle.

"Who's that?"

"Lexy is here. Say hi." Nans held the iPad up toward Lexy.

"Hi, Ida." Lexy waved.

"I hear you have another murder on your hands," Ida said.

Lexy nodded. She could see the sparkle of excitement in Ida's eyes on the screen. Ida, Nans and two of their friends delighted in solving murders and mysteries. They even had a name for themselves: the Ladies Detective Club.

The four of them lived in the Brooke Ridge Retirement Center and spent their days gathering clues and solving cases. The funny thing was, they rarely even left the complex because most of their detecting was done on their iPads. They'd been instrumental in helping Lexy solve a couple of murders she had inadvertently gotten involved in and even helped out the police department on a few cases.

Some women took up knitting in their golden years; the Ladies Detective Club liked to find killers and solve mysteries.

"Ruth found something interesting about your suspect...Aurea Pearce, was it?" Ida continued.

"Yes. Put her on." Nans put the tablet back on the table.

Lexy heard a shuffling sound coming from the device. She saw the screen blur then fill with Ruth's face.

"Hi Mona and Lexy," she said. Without waiting for a return greeting, she got right down to business. "I did a background check on Aurea Pearce. It seems she has some money troubles."

"Oh, really?" Nans exchanged an eyebrow-raised look with Lexy.

"She's maxed out on credit cards to the tune of $40,000 and is behind on house payments." The older woman leaned in closer, whispering into the iPad. "My sources tell me she has a gambling problem and may have taken out some unconventional loans."

"Excellent. Good work," Nans said.

"A gambling problem? Well she's come to the right place," Lexy said sarcastically, thinking that Las Vegas was the last place a person with a gambling problem should be.

Nans laughed. "Ain't that the truth. But if she's taken out unconventional loans, she might be getting pressure to pay them back quickly. Having a big win at the tables might save her from an undesirable fate."

"Or stacking the deck in the bakery contest to ensure she wins the $100,000 grand prize," Lexy pointed out.

"True," Nans said. "We have other suspects to look into, though."

"Helen is busy checking out the husband and looking into Judge Saunders's background. I'll call you back once we have something." Ruth said.

"OK, I'll fill you in on what we've found here then too. Bye." Nans pressed a button and the screen went blank.

She turned to Lexy, a gleam of satisfaction in her eyes. "Well, I'd say we just found a more pressing reason for Aurea Pearce to want to tip the scales in favor of her winning the contest. Maybe even one that would justify murder."

"Where are you off to tonight?" Lexy eyed her friend who was dressed in black leather pants, black leather ankle boots and a black T-shirt. Her pink tipped hair spiked up on top of her head like a birds plume.

"Poker tables," Cassie said, poking an earring into her ear to keep the five already there company. "You?"

"I'm going to play the slots. It will be nice to take a break from baking, but I'm not staying out late. I still have some finishing touches to put on those wedding cakes before the judging tomorrow afternoon."

"Yep, I'll be back early too. See you later then?"

Lexy nodded, watching Cassie shrug on a leather vest, then head out the door.

Assessing herself in the mirror she decided her faded jeans, pink tank top, and pink-striped platforms were perfect for a relaxing evening at the slot machines. Her hair was still a little wet from her shower, so she piled it on top of her head in a messy swirl.

She applied a few swipes of makeup, then followed Cassie out the door.

The elevator dumped her off in the casino. Scanning the room for a good place to lose her money, she spied a bank of progressive slot machines in the corner. She started off toward them but was stopped by a vibration in her back pocket. Her cell phone.

It was Jack. Her stomach clenched. Depending on what Jack had heard about the murder, the call might not go so well.

"Hi!" She answered with forced enthusiasm.

"Hey, how's it going out there?"

He didn't sound mad. So far so good.

"Great. I'm in second place," she said proudly.

"That's awesome. I'm so proud of you!"

Lexy felt her heart soar. *He was proud of her!*

"I got a message from a detective I know out there. Nikki Stone. Would you know what that's about?"

Her momentary happiness at his praise turned into dread, causing her soaring heart to sink like a stone.

"There was a little murder here..." She let her voice trail off, waiting for his response.

"A *little* murder?"

"One of the judges."

"Let me guess, *you* are somehow involved in the murder."

Lexy could hear impatience creeping into his voice.

"I found the body," she squeaked.

40

She heard him sigh on the other end. "Are you in trouble? Do I need to call Nikki right away?"

Lexy felt her heart clench upon hearing how easily the red headed detective's name rolled off his tongue. *Nikki*. She wondered what *kind* of relationship they had once had.

"No," she answered quickly. Calling Nik Stone was the last thing she wanted him to do. "Everything is all straightened out. I don't think Detective Stone needs to talk to you anymore."

"Oh, OK. Well what happened?"

"One of the judges was murdered. I just happened to find the body. I guess *someone* has to be the one to find them." She tried to make it sound like no big deal, then changed the subject. "How is Sprinkles?"

"Sprinkles is fine. We're having a great time, but we both miss you. Maybe I can get some time off work and come out there?"

Lexy felt a jolt of panic. She wanted to see Jack, but now wasn't a good time. He had been very clear during the last investigation that he took a dim view of her playing amateur detective.

She thought he was being a bit unfair. It's not like she went out looking for trouble. She just happened to get thrown into these situations that forced her to investigate. She was like a murder magnet.

Still, the last thing she needed was for him to come out and discover she was smack-dab in the middle of tracking down a killer. Or to get involved in it himself with Detective *Nikki* Stone.

"I miss you too. That would be great, but the contest schedule is really packed up until the end. I'm afraid I wouldn't have much time for you." She held her breath, waiting to see if he took the bait.

"Oh. I see. Well, it's probably just as well. I'm working on a big case here." Lexy felt her heart clench at the sound of disappointment in his voice.

"I'll be home in four days anyway; we can catch up on everything then. I can't wait to see you." She hoped he heard the sincerity in her voice.

"OK, sounds good. I'll talk to you later then," he said, then added, "So you're sure I don't have to call Nikki then?"

"Oh, I'm sure."

They hung up, and Lexy shoved the phone back into her pocket. Guilt washed over her. She tried to convince herself the little white lie was for the best. The contest schedule *was* pretty busy.

And she was sure the killer would be caught soon and she would be cleared. Once it was over, she could return to her normally blissful life with Jack and Sprinkles in Brooke Ridge Falls.

Unless the police didn't catch the real killer by the time the contest was over.

She thought about how Aurea's trouble with money gave her a good motive, but she wasn't one hundred percent convinced Aurea was the killer. She knew from the last murder case she had been involved in that sometimes things are not what they seem. She needed to rule out some of the other suspects before she could be confident that Aurea was the culprit.

She continued toward the slot machines passing the same bar where she had seen Amanda Scott-Saunders's husband earlier. She glanced into the bar, wondering if she should pop in for a little drink. *He was in there again!*

Recognizing a perfect opportunity to do some more investigative gathering, Lexy pivoted on her heels, changing her course to head straight for the bar.

Chapter Six

The bar was practically empty. A couple sat at a table in the corner flirting. A woman sat alone at one end of the bar. At the other end sat Peter Saunders.

Lexy hopped up onto a plush gray microfiber bar stool one seat away from Saunders.

"What can I get you?" The bartender slid a napkin in front of Lexy.

"A White Russian with a splash of Coke, please." Lexy stole a sideways glance at Peter Saunders and caught him looking at her.

"Hi." She smiled at him.

He nodded a greeting. "You look familiar."

"I'm in the *Bakery Battles* contest." She tilted her head in the direction of Bakery Battles Stadium. "Do I know you from there?"

"Oh, probably. My wife is...I mean, *was* a judge." He looked down at his drink. Lexy thought she saw the gleam of a tear in the corner of his eye.

"You're Peter Saunders?" she asked.

He nodded, still staring down at the drink.

"I'm so sorry for your loss." She stuck her hand out toward him. "Lexy Baker."

He stared at her hand, then made a half hearted attempt at shaking it.

"Thanks," he said dully, then picked up his glass draining it in one gulp. He motioned at the bartender for a refill. Judging by the way he swayed on the chair, it wasn't the first refill he'd had either.

Lexy sipped her own drink. She had forgotten to eat supper, and the alcohol made a beeline for her brain, emboldening her.

"I just don't understand why anyone would want to do that," Lexy said.

"Me either. I mean, Mandy could be a bit abrasive and some people really didn't like her, but you don't kill someone just because you don't like them."

"Are you holding up okay? I mean, you must really be in shock. You guys were very close." Lexy fished for information on their relationship.

"We've been married for ten years, but lately things have been a little strained. We had some money troubles. We had been fighting a lot, but I still loved her..." His voice trailed off.

"All couples fight, and most have money troubles at times too."

"She said everything was going to be okay with the money. I didn't know what she meant." He rubbed his face with his hands.

"Did you notice Amanda acting strangely at all?" she blurted out.

Peter turned his head toward her, his eyes squinting. "Strangely? She was acting kind of... secretive. Quiet. Distant. I wondered if, well..."

"She was having an affair?" Lexy prompted.

Saunders's shoulders sagged and he nodded.

"Was she?" Lexy took another sip.

"She said she wasn't. We argued about it. She swore nothing was going on, but a few times she left the room early - I'm not sure she was going where she *said* she was going. Even that morning..."

"Didn't that make you mad?"

"What?" Peter narrowed his eyes at Lexy, his body stiffening.

"Did you get along after you argued, or did things simmer?" The alcohol encouraged her to persist against her better judgement.

Peter stood up, knocking over his drink in the process. "What's with these questions? I already answered them for the police!"

Lexy couldn't help herself. She had to ask., "Where were you when your wife was murdered?"

46

Peter Saunders's face turned beet-red. "Are you accusing me?" he shouted, then took a step toward Lexy, reaching out to grab her.

She jumped up from her chair stepping out of his reach. His outstretched arms flailed toward her. In his drunken state, he misjudged the distance and stumbled forward, causing Lexy to jump back - bumping into, and almost knocking over, Detective Jake Ryan.

"Whoa, whoa. What's going on here?" Jake stepped between Lexy and Peter holding his hands up to keep them apart.

Peter pointed at Lexy. "She accused me of murder!"

"I did not. I simply asked where you were when your wife was killed." Lexy crossed her arms over her chest.

"OK, I'm sure you're both upset about the murder but let's leave the detecting to the police." He glared at Lexy. "We don't know who killed Mrs. Saunders, but we're working on it."

Detective Ryan's speech seemed to diffuse Peter's anger. "Fine, but keep *her* away from me."

He jerked his head in Lexy's direction, then stomped back to his seat at the bar.

Lexy looked up at the detective, expecting to get the same lecture Jack usually gave her. Instead she saw him smiling down at her.

"Wanna have a seat?" He gestured toward one of the small tables.

"Sure," Lexy said glancing over at the bar toward her drink.

His eyes followed her glance. "We can get you a new one," he said, then put his hand on the small of her back, leading her over to a table.

Detective Ryan held out a chair, and Lexy plopped into it. She stared across the table at him. She recognized him from the murder scene - the *nice* detective who had questioned her first.

But she must have been preoccupied then because she hadn't noticed his boyish good looks. His straight white teeth must have cost a fortune. They were the perfect accessory to his chiseled jaw, which wore a bit of five o'clock shadow giving his baby face a hint of danger. Lexy thought one could easily get lost in his blue eyes.

"Do you want another drink?" He jolted her out of her daze.

Lexy gave herself a mental head shake. She already felt a bit tipsy from her first drink.

Considering the way her stomach fluttered when she looked at Detective Ryan, she had better not.

"Just a coffee, please."

He disappeared in the direction of the bar, returning in a few minutes with a beer for himself and a coffee for her.

"Thanks. I don't think I got your first name?" Lexy peered at him over the rim of her coffee cup.

"Jake. Jake Ryan."

Lexy smiled at him. "You probably already know my name, I guess. Lexy Baker."

He laughed. Lexy noticed his voice had a rich timbre one could easily get used to. "Yes, the body-finding baker."

Lexy shrugged. "What can I say, I have a knack for finding bodies."

She looked over at Peter Saunders, who was back in his chair with a fresh drink. "Speaking of which, do you think Saunders did it?"

"What do you think?" Jake held her gaze with his baby blues. Lexy wasn't all too happy about the fluttering effect this had on her stomach. She took a sip of coffee, hoping the sobering effect of the coffee would stop the fluttering.

"There's some talk she may have been having an affair. Maybe Saunders found out and killed her in a fit of passion?"

49

"Well, the strangulation could indicate a crime of passion, but there's no hard evidence to suggest it was him."

"Do you guys have any idea who it was?" Lexy asked.

"We're still sifting through the information. So far, we've ruled out most of the contestants because we could verify they were in their rooms at the time. We're going through all the surveillance tapes in the casino and hotel now, so we'll know who the killer is shortly."

Lexy remembered the confession of Aurea's room-mate. *Should she tell him?*

"Am I a suspect?" She tried putting on her most innocent face. It usually worked with Jack - hopefully Detective Ryan was no different.

Jake laughed. "Well, a lot of the evidence we have right now *does* point to you, but once we sift through all the video tapes I'm sure that will prove you couldn't have done it."

Lexy watched the steam from her coffee waver as she breathed out a sigh of relief. *They didn't think she had done it.* She took another sip.

"I talked to some of the other bakers to see if they noticed anything unusual, and I found something that might be useful to you." Jake leaned forward, his eyes narrowing with interest. "Go on."

"Aurea Pearce - she's one of the contestants - her roommate said Aurea left the room at 3:25 that morning."

"Really? I don't remember her telling *us* that."

"She said she just told you Aurea left *before* she did, but not the exact time. I hope I didn't get her into trouble."

"No. Thanks for telling me. That's important to know." Jake took a swig from his beer. Lexy realized he had hardly touched it. "Do you have a cell phone?" he asked.

Lexy nodded. Jake held out his hand, and she dug it out of her pocket and handed it over.

"I'm going to put my cell number in here. If you hear any other interesting information, will you call and let me know?"

Lexy wasn't sure how to answer. *Did he really want to know if she found anything out, or was his number an invitation for something else?* She decided she didn't want to know.

"OK." She watched him punch in his number, then reached out for the phone. He handed it back, brushing his finger tips against hers.

Thankfully, the coffee had done it's job of keeping her clear headed, and she successfully ignored the tingle in her hand.

Is this the sort of thing that happened with Amanda Scott-Saunders and Evan Westmore?

Lexy stood up. "Well, Detective, thanks for the coffee. I'd better be going now."

Jake stood, his mostly full beer still on the table.

"It was nice talking to you, Ms. Baker. Don't forget to call if you find anything else out."

"Oh, I won't," Lexy said, then left the bar, heading toward the casino. She didn't go straight to the slot machine she had been aiming for originally though; the conversation with Saunders had given her an idea.

She headed for Bakery Battles Stadium. If Amanda and Evan Westmore were having an affair, that might give Peter or Evan a motive for killing Amanda.

The question was, were they having an affair? She didn't know for sure, but she had an idea where she might be able to find a clue.

###

Skirting the edge of the casino, Lexy took the back hallway toward Bakery Battles Stadium. The dim lighting in the empty stadium area gave the large room a sinister ambiance. Lexy forced herself forward, jabbing her finger into her eye to keep it from twitching.

She took the middle hallway toward the back where the offices were. Her footsteps echoed hollowly in the empty room.

Clack. Clack. Clack.

Scuff.

What was that?

Lexy whirled around. *Was someone behind her?*

No one was there.

"Hello?" she called out tentatively. No one answered.

She gave a little laugh. *Silly me, getting all spooked by an empty room.*

Lexy turned back around. She willed herself to keep facing forward as she picked up the pace to the back of the room.

The offices were makeshift rooms separated by temporary walls. Each had its own door, but there were no locks so every office was accessible. She found Evan Westmore's and turned the knob.

The door clicked open. Taking one last backward glance, Lexy slipped into the office, then silently closed the door.

Dim light from the stadium filtered in through opaque glass slots at the very top of the walls, giving the office a dusk-like feel. Slats of light reflected dust motes suspended in the air.

Looking around, Lexy realized she had no idea what she was looking for.

An antique mahogany desk sat in the middle of the room. *Pretty ritzy for a temporary office.* Behind it, a book-case with neatly stacked books. To the left, a filing cabinet.

Lexy tried the filing cabinet drawers. Locked. She moved over to the desk. The top was neatly arraigned with a desk pad, onyx pen set, and a gorgeous pair of onyx book ends. Westmore certainly had expensive taste. Lexy wondered how much the event coordinator position paid.

In the center of the desk, she spotted some blank personalized stationary papers with matching envelopes. Lexy ran her fingertips over the paper. She had an affinity for good-quality paper, and this particular stock was extraordinary.

She lifted a piece. It was heavy. Handmade with an interesting texture. Probably mulberry paper - only a few places even made this type of paper. She knew it was very expensive.

Replacing the paper, she took care to line it up exactly as it had been. Sinking into the high-backed desk chair, she heard the soft tufted leather make a puffing sound.

Starting in the middle drawer, she leafed through the contents. It held the usual stuff - pens, pencils, notes, paper, some personal photos including one of Westmore in a tux standing next to another man in a tux, their arms linked together. Lexy saw the happy smile on the normally dour man's face and mused at what the occasion might be.

Muffled sounds filtered into the room, increasing her anxiety. She cast a nervous glance at the door. Getting caught in there would probably result in her being kicked out of the competition. She didn't want to stay any longer than necessary, so she sped up her search even though her nervous eye twitch was making it difficult to see.

Hidden under a stack of papers in the bottom right drawer she found what she was looking for. A small black leather date book. Inside were cryptic messages written on various days. Just the thing someone who was having an affair might keep.

Lexy shoved the book into her back pocket and stood up. Replacing the chair to its exact position she looked around the office to make sure everything looked the way it had when she entered.

A noise in the hallway outside made the hair on the back of her neck stand up. She tiptoed over to the door. Cracking it open, she peered out. The hallway was empty. She slipped out the door, holding the knob as she closed it so it wouldn't make a sound, then hurried down the hall and out into the main corridor to the casino.

Chapter Seven

"You saw her going into Westmore's office?" Nik raised her eyebrows at Jake.

"Yep. I followed her into the stadium after hours and she went straight to his office. Seemed like she didn't want anyone following her either."

"Did she see you?"

Nik saw a flash of Jake's dimples. "Come on, Nik, you know I know how to follow someone without being seen."

Nik turned to the board they had laid out with suspects' names, pictures and data. "Why, would she be going to Westmore's office?"

"I'm not sure. When I saw her in the bar, she was having words with Peter Saunders about the victim and Westmore having an affair."

"They were?" Nik turned to look at him.

"Yeah, Saunders looked like he was going to hit her."

"No, I mean Westmore and the victim - they were having an affair?"

"Oh...Lexy said there were rumors about that, but I haven't heard anything."

Nik wrinkled her brow. Turning back to the board, she drew a line from Evan Westmore to

Amanda Saunders with a question mark in between.

"We better check that out. It still doesn't answer the question of why Baker would be going there."

Jake rubbed his chin. "It looked like she didn't want anyone to see her there - maybe they were having a secret meeting."

Nik picked up a manilla folder from the desk and held it out toward Jake. "This is the folder on Westmore - seems he was into some shady business."

She watched Jake thumb through the folder. "I wonder how he got the event coordinator job with a track record like this?"

Nik shrugged. "Who knows. He's never done anything even close to murder, but he appears to be quite the swindler."

"Do you think Lexy Baker and Evan Westmore are running some kind of scam together? Maybe Saunders got in the way?"

"It's possible. What did you tell her before she went to his office?" Nik asked.

"Just that we were weeding through the surveillance tapes and would soon know who the killer was...do you think she went to warn Westmore?"

Nik screwed up her face, thinking about it. "We need to find out more about Lexy Baker. Too bad my contact in the police department in her town hasn't called me back. Baker and her grandmother claim they actually helped bring in the killer from the murders she was messed up in: I wonder if it was to cover their own tracks or if they really are just amateur crime fighters."

"There's another thing she told me that was very interesting."

Nik invited him to elaborate by raising her eyebrows.

"She said Aurea Pearce's roommate told her that Aurea left the room at 3:25. That would mean she was out of the room at the time of the murder. *And* that she lied to us about when she left the room."

"Aurea Pearce is Lexy's strongest competitor. She would have a strong motive to get her kicked out of the competition...or arrested."

"Yeah, a $100,000 motive. But Pearce also had a motive to get rid of Saunders."

"Oh?"

"With Saunders gone, a new judge will have to be named from the pool of alternate judges. One of those judges happens to be good friends with Aurea Pearce."

"We better check that out too. Find out what room Pearce is in and put a rush on looking at the surveillance tapes for that area. See if you can find out when she left and where she went. And keep a close watch on Lexy Baker - whether she's up to something or not, her amateur investigating could lead you to some interesting clues."

"You two stayed out awfully late last night." Lexy stood in the middle of their hotel room, looking at Cassie and Nans.

"I won $500 on a jackpot, so I wanted to keep playing," Nans said. Her bright green eyes sparkled as she pulled a wad of money out of her purse to show them.

"I was on a roll at the poker tables. Kind of hard to leave when the cards are going your way. You were fast asleep when I got in," Cassie said.

"I got something even better than money last night." Lexy reached into her jeans pocket and pulled out the little black date book.

"What's that?" Cassie held out her hand.

Lexy felt her cheeks grow pink. "I kind of found myself alone in Evan Westmore's office and it just happened to find its way into my pocket."

"You stole it?" Nans asked.

Lexy nodded.

"Lexy! If you get caught you'll probably get kicked out of the competition," Cassie said in wide-eyed shock.

"I know, but I ran into Peter Saunders in the bar. He got so mad when I mentioned that Evan Westmore and his wife might have been having an affair, I wanted to see if I could find any evidence to prove it."

"Yeah, I heard that rumor. They were seen meeting, and she was dressing all spiffy." Cassie opened the book. "But this is gibberish - it doesn't prove anything."

Nans put her hand out for the book. "Let me see."

Cassie handed it over. Nans looked at it carefully, slowly turning the pages. "It might not look like much to the untrained eye because it's in some sort of code. I bet Ida can make sense of it though. She used to be a cryptographer."

Nans reached for her iPad. A few keystrokes later the device made a ringing noise, then Ida's face appeared on the screen.

"Hi!"

"Hi, Ida, we have something interesting for you today." Nans held the book up to the camera so Ida could see it on her iPad screen. "This book seems to have entries in code - can you decipher it?"

Ida squinted on the other end of the screen. "I think so. Can you take pictures of it and email them to me?"

"Sure." Nans put the book down and dug in her purse for her cell phone. "Did you find anything out about the Saunders?"

"Not much. They have a modest house, make a modest income. Have a bit of debt, but who doesn't these days? The husband is an accountant. There are some recent high credit card charges recently on Amanda's card - high-end clothing stores and boutiques."

Lexy remembered the fancy purses and clothes Saunders had started wearing. *Did she buy them to impress Westmore?*

Lexy watched Nans quickly snap off some pictures of the little black book, then send them off to Ida's phone.

"Did you find any reports of violence or fighting?" Lexy shouted at the iPad.

"No, they were a model couple. And you don't need to shout, dear - I'm not deaf."

"I just emailed those pictures to you," Nans said.

"Oh, great. Hold on." Ida disappeared from the screen, then reappeared with her cell phone in hand. Lexy, Cassie, and Nans stared silently at the screen while they watched her page through the photos.

"Well?" Nans said, finally.

"It's definitely some sort of code - it looks like something to do with numbers of some sort. I'll need some time to decode it properly to be able to tell you more. I'm also working on a police case for Jack, so it might be a day or two."

"I was hoping it was some sort of diary or record of his liasons with Amanda Scott-Saunders," Lexy said.

"I'm not sure if it is or isn't." Ida looked thoughtful. "But one thing I am sure of, Westmore had a secret that was important enough for him to want to record it, but damaging enough that he didn't want anyone else to know about it."

"We better hurry, I want to put some finishing touches on the wedding cakes before the judging." Lexy held the door open to their suite and pushed Cassie through.

The girls sprinted for the elevator, straightening their aprons on the way down.

When the elevator stopped on the bottom floor, they rushed out, making their way toward the back hall that led to the stadium.

"I wish we had more free time to enjoy Vegas," Lexy said glancing in at the casino wistfully. Even at this early hour, it was humming with activity.

Cassie nodded. "We should have booked a couple of extra days. I feel like we hardly have enough time to get our baking done for the contest with the time we do have."

Lexy listened to their shoes make clacking noises on the tile floor. The contest was on a tight schedule. Each day there was a new challenge that they would be judged on, which meant they only had 24 hours to come up with something extraordinary. That didn't leave much time for fun and games.

"At least our hard work is paying off," she said.

"Yes, its cool that we are in the top tier of the contest. A few bakers have already packed up and gone home."

After every challenge, the bottom ten percent of bakers were eliminated and sent home. The competition kept getting smaller and smaller, and tougher and tougher. Luckily Lexy usually ended up placing in the top three of each challenge, which was important since the scores from each challenge were added up at the end to determine the final winner.

Reaching their kitchen booth, Lexy could see that the other booths were already starting fill up with bakers and their assistants, all busy working out their finishing touches for the wedding cake challenge.

"You get the cakes out and I'll grab the spatulas." Lexy rushed over to the wire rack that held their equipment while Cassie opened the doors of the large fridge.

"Lexy...You better look at this."

Lexy spun around, hearing her friends voice rise in panic.

"What?" she started over towards the fridge, then stopped short when she saw the cause of Cassie's panic.

Inside sat the wedding cake they had labored over for the competition.

Ruined.

One of her very own giant butcher's knives stuck out of the center, the words "Back Off" in red food coloring written all over her beautiful white cake.

Chapter Eight

Lexy stared at the cake, her stomach sinking like it was filled with lead. *Who could have done this?*

Cassie turned around, wide-eyed. "What should we do?"

"I wonder if we can fix it," Lexy said, fighting back tears. Without the cake, she'd be disqualified from this part of the competition, severely limiting her chances of winning.

She whipped her cell phone out of her pocket, snapping off a few pictures of the cake.

"Whoever did this either wants me to stop investigating the murder or wants to ruin my chances of winning Bakery Battles...or both." Lexy glanced over at Aurea Pearce's kitchen. It was empty.

"You need to tell the police. Isn't the cake some sort of evidence?" Cassie asked.

"Probably, but I took pictures and that's going to have to be good enough. I'm not losing this competition because someone sabotaged our cake." Lexy moved over to the fridge, holding the door wider. "Let's get the cake out onto the table and see what we can do with it."

Cassie slid her hand under the cake while Lexy held the door. Lexy noticed something falling to the floor as Cassie moved the cake out.

Dust?

No. Glitter.

Lexy looked at her hands - tiny dots of glitter sparkled in the harsh stadium lighting.

"Cassie, did you put glitter on the cake?"

"No, why?"

"There's glitter here over by the fridge and on the handle."

"That's strange I don't think we even *have* any glitter, do we?"

Lexy rubbed her hands together, watching the shiny flakes drop to the floor. "No, must have been someone else - a cleaning person maybe?"

Lexy watched Cassie edge the cake onto the table, her mind already whirling with ideas on how to fix it. But first, she looked up Detective Jake Ryan's number on her phone and sent him the cake pictures with a text of what she had found. At least they couldn't say she didn't tell them about it, and she could always act dumb about touching the cake.

"Let's take the knife out, but be careful with the handle - we don't want to smudge any fingerprints."

The girls slipped on the latex gloves they normally wore when preparing food. Cassie gingerly grabbed the end of the knife, sliding it carefully out of the cake. She put it out of the way on the corner of the long table.

Whipping up some frosting, they set about repairing the cake - patching up the big hole and carefully covering the red words with white frosting.

"We better speed it up." Lexy nodded toward the other end of the stadium where the judges were already doing a preliminary judging on the cakes.

She glanced over at the next booth. Aurea Pearce had arrived. She was setting her cakes out on pedestals, applying some finishing touches.

Aurea looked over at Lexy and smirked. Lexy wondered if it was an "I ruined your cake" smirk. She craned her neck to see if Aurea had any glitter in her booth.

Working at breakneck speed, Lexy and Cassie managed to make the cake presentable. They put the two cakes out on presentation platters at the front of their booth just in the nick of time.

The judges were at Aurea's booth. Lexy noticed that the judge in Amanda Scott-Saunders's spot was Grace Harvey and her heart took a nosedive. She wasn't surprised when Harvey heaped praise on Aurea's cakes or when Aurea cast another smirk in her direction as the judges moved toward Lexy's booth.

Lexy held her breath, watching the judges bend over her cake stand inspect them from every angle.

"This one looks a little funny," Grace Harvey said to the other two judges.

Lexy watched silently as they all bent down and peered at the cake sideways. Out of the corner of her eye she could see Detective Jake Ryan approaching. She hoped he had the good sense to stay back while the judges were there.

"A little off-center, but its not too distracting. Still, you'll get points off for it. But the roses are beautiful." Tim Gartner, the head judge, pointed at the roses with his pen.

"The grooms cake is fantastic." Joan Lutner, the aesthetics judge, smiled at Lexy.

Lexy nodded her thanks, then breathed a sigh of relief as they moved on. They would judge all the cakes for appearance, then the best four would be selected for the tasting judgment.

Jake Ryan moved in to fill the void left by the judges.

"Where's the cake?" He held up his phone, pointing to the picture Lexy had sent him earlier.

Lexy put on her wide-eyed innocent look. Nodding toward the cake on the table, she said, "We had to repair it for the judging...but we saved you the knife."

She went over to the table where they had put the knife. Picking it up by the edge with her thumb and forefinger, she held it up for Jake to inspect.

He whipped out an evidence bag, indicating for Lexy to put the knife in.

"I wish you hadn't tampered with the cake. That's evidence."

"Oh, sorry." Lexy tried batting her eyelashes but only ended up aggravating her eye twitch.

She saw Jake looking down at the cake, comparing it to the picture on his phone. She was afraid he was going to insist on taking it when the judges returned.

"Good news," Tim informed her, "you made fourth place, so go ahead and move your cakes over to the tasting area.

Lexy turned to Cassie, and the girls high-fived each other. "We did it!" Lexy felt her heart soar. It only became slightly deflated when she heard Tim telling Aurea she had won second place. Hopefully

Lexy's cakes tasted better than Aurea's which, could give her an overall win.

Ignoring Jake, she grabbed a wheeled cart and carefully transferred the cakes onto it while Cassie ran over to the rack to grab cake plates, forks, and a cake knife. With the cart loaded, the girls took off for the tasting area, leaving Jake in their wake.

Lexy felt her stomach do nervous flip-flops as she took her place in the row of contestants directly across from the judges, who were seated at a long table. Each contestant had sliced bite-size pieces from their cakes, which were resting on identical stainless steel carts in front of them.

Lexy looked at her cart. Slices of the white bride's cake oozed raspberry liqueur filling. She had been careful not to cut into the damaged side of the cake so as not to bring attention to the patch job she and Cassie had done to hide the sabotage. The groom's cake looked equally delicious with its hazelnut toffee filling shining in between the chocolate layers. Lexy took a deep, calming breath and her nose was treated to a variety of sweet smells from the raspberry, caramel, and chocolate.

Evan Westmore made his way to the podium. Lexy noticed he was wearing an Armani suit. The man had good taste if nothing else. He posed for the cameras that were rolling to record the judging and began to speak.

"It's with great sadness that I announce the death of one of our judges, Amanda Scott-Saunders. She was a wonderful judge and a great personal friend." Lexy studied Westmore as he went on to say a few words about Saunders. How *close* of a personal friend was she? Lexy wondered.

"And now, I'd like to announce our new judge —Grace Harvey." Lexy noticed Aurea looking at her with a "cat that ate the canary" smile.

Lexy tuned Westmore out as he droned on about Grace Harvey's qualifications and, then introduced the rest of the judges and contestants. She looked around at all of them wondering if one could be the murderer.

The judges went through the cakes one by one tasting and critiquing the flavors of each. Lexy got high marks for her flavor combinations, but was it enough to overcome the points off for the damaged cake and take the overall win?

Westmore collected the scorecards from the judges, did a little bit of math, then cleared his throat to announce the winners.

"In third place, winning four points for aesthetics and four points for taste, is Bill Salida." Lexy clapped along with everyone else as the rotund baker went up to collect his ribbon.

"In second place, winning five points for aesthetics and four points for taste is-" Westmore paused for effect, and Lexy found herself holding her breath. "Aurea Pearce!"

Lexy looked over at Aurea and found her glaring at Grace Harvey. She noticed Aurea's face was bright red as she went up, snatched the ribbon out of Westmore's hand, then stomped off toward the kitchen area.

Lexy let her breath out. That meant the winner was either her or Corinne.

Lexy knew the judges had liked the taste of her cakes, but the problems with the damaged white cake worried her. At least she could take solace in the fact that Aurea hadn't gotten first place.

Lexy would actually be happy to see the blue ribbon for this judging go to Corinne. She knew she had enough points to pull ahead in the other segments of the contest, and besides she had taken a liking to Corinne and was very sympathetic to her money problems and the fact that she was pursing her dream even though her husband left her broke and with young children to raise.

Westmore looked down from his podium at Lexy and Corinne like a bird singling out its prey. Lexy thought she saw him give her an angry glare, but maybe it was just the lighting.

"That means either Lexy or Corinne is the winner of the wedding cake contest." Westmore stated the obvious. "-and...the...winner...is"

Lexy and Corinne glanced at each other nervously.

"Corinne Conners!"

The room burst out in applause. Lexy found herself clapping the loudest because she was genuinely happy for her friend. She ran over and threw her arms around Corinne, who was wiping away tears.

She admired the winning cakes up close; they were beautiful. Tall and elegant, the designs meticulously blending contemporary with traditional.

Lexy felt her heart swell for the young baker... until she noticed something about the cakes that made her feel like she'd been punched in the gut.

The cakes were covered in glitter - the same type of glitter Lexy had found near the sabotaged cake in her kitchen.

Chapter Nine

"Did you see Corrine's cake? It was loaded with glitter!" Lexy whispered to Cassie as they made their way back to their kitchen.

Cassie stopped short. "Oh my God. You mean like the glitter we found near our white cake?"

Lexy nodded. "Do you think Corinne sabotaged the cake? Maybe to knock me out of the competition, or because she's the murderer and wants me to stop looking into it?"

Cassie shrugged. "I don't know, but either way I'd watch myself if I were you."

"Yeah, we may have just added another suspect to the list. I'm going to give Nans a call and see what the ladies can dig up on Corinne."

Lexy took out her cell phone and punched in Nans' number, then listened impatiently to it ring several times. "Damn it, she's probably in the casino and can't hear the phone. I'll have to text her."

Lexy fumbled with the keyboard typing out a quick text for Nans.

"Who are you texting?"

Lexy jumped at the voice, which was awfully close to her ear. She whirled around and her heart sped up when she saw Detective Jake Ryan had snuck up on her and was standing dangerously close. *Had he seen the text?*

"I'm just texting my grandmother." Lexy considered telling Jake about Corinne's glitter cakes, but something held her back. She wasn't positive Corinne had anything to do with the cake sabotage and didn't want to get her in trouble with the police.

"Did you win?" Jake asked, nodding his head in the direction of the cakes.

"No, I didn't win this one," Lexy said ruefully. "We couldn't repair the cake fully and lost quite a few points because it wasn't up to par."

"Oh, sorry." Jake looked genuinely sorry, which made Lexy's heart do a little hop, skip and jump against her will.

He ventured on. "I had them check the knife really quick. There are no prints on it. Do you have any idea who could've done this?"

"No." Lexy felt the nervous tic in her eye start up. She was glad it was Detective Jake Ryan and not Detective Jack Perillo in front of her. Jack would recognize the eye tic as a sure sign she wasn't telling the whole truth.

"I guess maybe someone wants to scare me out of the competition."

"Or maybe the murderer doesn't like you running around asking questions," Jake offered.

Lexy's thoughts went immediately to Peter Saunders. He *had* been pretty angry with her, and the attack on the cake sure seemed like an expression of anger - maybe the glitter *was* just a coincidence.

"That could be," she said, thinking that if Jack were here, he'd be giving her the same exact reproachful look Jake was.

Jake nodded. "Well, I think you'd better watch your back, it looks like someone might be out to get you."

Lexy felt a chill run up her spine, causing her body to vibrate. It took her a second to realize the vibrations were from her cell phone. She dug it out of her pocket thinking it might be Nans. It was Jack.

She glanced up at Jake "Sorry, I have to take this."

"OK, I'll talk to you later. Be careful." Jake turned and she watched him walk to the exit door. Lexy sucked in a deep breath before she answered her phone.

She was glad Jack couldn't see her eye twitching nervously at the little white lies - more like omissions - she was about to tell him. If Jack found out about the sabotaged cake, he'd be out here in a flash or, worse, he'd try to make her come home.

#

"What do you mean she covered up the cake?" Nik stared at Jake, the crease between her brows deepening.

"When I got there, they had already repaired the damage. She said she needed the cake for the wedding cake challenge otherwise she would've been disqualified."

"So she was more worried about the challenge than the fact that somebody deliberately sabotaged her cake? Does that seem a little odd to you?"

"Yeah, most people are more concerned about their safety. She didn't seem upset about the threat at all."

Nik pursed her lips. "Do you think she staged it? You know, to throw us off track and deflect the suspicion from her?"

Jake shrugged. "It's possible...the knife was from her kitchen, but the perpetrator could have just grabbed the closest knife. I don't think she did it though. I think someone really wanted to warn her off of something."

Nik's eyes narrowed. "Don't tell me you're getting sweet on our little baker?"

Jake laughed. "No, it's just a gut instinct."

"Detective Stone, take a look at this."

Nik heard the voice of Detective Ducat on the other side of the room.

She turned her head in his direction, her eyes drawn to a large television screen where one of the surveillance tapes from the casino was playing. It showed one of the poker tables. Seated right in the middle was Aurea Pearce.

Nik moved closer to the screen. "That's Aurea Pearce." She looked at the timestamp on the right corner of the screen. "The time indicates she was there at 3:31 am. Is this tape from the morning of the murder?"

Ducat nodded.

"How long was she there?"

"She played until 6 am."

Nik turned to Jake. "Well I guess we can scratch one suspect off our list. Aurea Pearce couldn't possibly be the killer-she was seen on a time stamped tape playing poker when Amanda Scott-Saunders was killed."

"I found something else you might be interested in," Ducat said.

Nik watched impatiently while Ducat hunted around on the computer for another recording.

"Here it is." He punched a few buttons, and the screen showed the entrance to *Bakery Battles* Stadium. "This is from last night."

Nick watched Lexy Baker appear on screen, open the doors to the stadium, then disappear inside. A few seconds later Jake appeared, following her in.

Ducat fast-forwarded the replay four minutes, and another figure appeared on the screen-Evan Westmore. Nik watched him open the door, cast a furtive glance behind him, and then slip into the stadium.

"That's Westmore!" Jake said.

Nik felt the exciting rush of finding a new clue energize her body.

"Yeah, and he's going into the stadium right behind Lexy Baker." She turned to Jake. "Looks like our theory about them having a secret meeting might just prove to be true."

Jake frowned. "Yes, but if that's true, why didn't I see him go past me?"

Nik shrugged. "Who knows? Maybe there is another way to get to his office. If only there were cameras inside the stadium, then we'd know for sure."

Jake stared at the screen dubiously. "Or maybe he went in there for something else..."

Nik went back over to the board filled with suspects and crossed off Aurea Pearce's name.

"So we have Evan Westmore, Peter Saunders, and Lexy Baker." She stared at the board, tapping her finger on her lower lip. "We don't have anything solid on any of them, but Baker keeps turning up in the middle of everything, which makes me rather suspicious of her."

"Yeah, but what is her motive? For Westmore and Saunders we have the affair angle. If Amanda *was* having an affair with Westmore, either peter or Evan could have killed her in a fit of passion."

"Yes, but we have yet to prove there even *was* an affair."

"Right, it seems like we are missing something big-the *real* motive for the murder," Jake said.

"I think it's time to turn up the heat on our little baker friend. I want you to tell her we've eliminated Aurea Pearce and that our suspect list is down to three, including her. If she knows something, or is involved, it might make her nervous and cause her to get careless. Maybe she will slip up somehow, lead us to the truth, and help us close this case."

Nik punctuated the last 3 words by ramming the top down onto her whiteboard marker.

She turned to Jake. "I want you to stick to her like glue. Put a couple of other detectives on her so we can watch her 24/7 - I have a feeling our little baker girl is about to make her move."

Chapter Ten

Lexy looked out the window of their hotel room. It was an exceptionally clear day and their tenth floor room offered a phenomenal view. To the left she could see the giant pyramid of the Luxor hotel, to the right she could see the mountain range. Below, the people moved like ants scurrying back and forth between the various hotels.

She sighed, wishing she had more time to explore the other hotels and casinos, but the contest schedule was fairly tight and there was this nasty murder business going on. She had little time today for anything other than making pies for the second to last challenge in *Bakery Battles*. She had to really step up her game to overtake Aurea Pearce.

The ringing of the iPad interrupted her thoughts, tearing her attention from the majestic view.

"Hello girls!" Nans greeted Ida, Ruth, and Helen whose faces could be seen clustered around the iPad screen.

"How are things in Vegas? It's cold and snowing here," Ida said.

"Wonderful." Nans took the iPad over to the window, holding it up to the glass. "Look at the view we have today!"

The three ladies on the other end made the appropriate noises of appreciation. Nans left the window and took the iPad back to the table. "Now, tell us what you found out."

Cassie, Lexy, and Nans clustered around the tablet. Lexy couldn't help but picture them being a mostly younger mirror image of the three ladies on the other side.

Ruth's face took over the iPad screen. "I made an interesting discovery about your friend Corinne. It seems foreclosure proceedings were recently started on her house."

Lexy felt her heart clench for the other woman. She couldn't imagine how that must feel with three kids and a run-away husband. Then she realized that staving off the foreclosure was a powerful motive for taking drastic measures to win the contest.

"That *is* interesting...it could give her a motive to ruin my cake, but I don't know if it would be something she would kill over." Lexy bit her lower lip thoughtfully.

Ruth's face was replaced by Ida's. "I had a chance to look at the pages from that book."

Lexy glanced nervously at the drawer beside her bed where she had stashed it. Somehow she had to get the book back to Evan Westmore's office.

"And?"

"It looks like a series of numbers and dates," Ida said. "Large numbers like twelve thousand, five thousand, and so on - the dates are fairly recent. At least that's what it looks like if I've done the decoding properly."

"Numbers and dates?" Lexy repeated, her eyebrows mashed together in confusion.

"Yes, dear, that's what I said."

"I was thinking it would be some sort of record of Evan's rendezvous with Amanda Scott-Saunders. Maybe some notes about when they met and where?"

Ida worried her bottom lip. "I don't think so, unless my calculations are way off."

Lexy felt her stomach sink. Proof of the affair would help to finger either Westmore or Peter Saunders as the killer. She was hoping there might be an entry for the morning of Amanda Saunders's death, but no such luck.

She could hear Ruth vying for the iPad on the other end and watched the dizzying image on the screen as the iPad was passed from Ida to Ruth.

"I think you're barking up the wrong tree with that theory, Lexy," Ruth said.

"Oh, why is that?" Lexy, Nans, and Cassie all exchanged a look.

"I did some checking on Westmore's background and I think you can safely rule out the notion of him having an affair with Amanda Scott-Saunders-Evan Westmore is gay."

"I hope Nans is okay doing some surveillance on Corinne. I would've done it myself, but I have so much work here." Lexy spread her arms to indicate their kitchen in Bakery Battles Stadium.

Cassie placed two large bowls on the baking table and pulled a stand mixer out from the corner. "Are you kidding? She lives for this stuff. She'll be fine. Besides, we need this win to recover from the disastrous wedding cake challenge."

"I know, there's only one challenge left after this and we need all the points we can get to win the contest, since the points from all the challenges are added up to determine the overall winner." Lexy went over to the refrigerator and started piling her arms high with eggs, butter, and milk.

She dropped the ingredients onto the counter near Cassie, then went over to her pantry area for flour and sugar. The pantry was next to Aurea Pearce's kitchen. She couldn't help but sneak a peek through the wire shelving to see what Aurea was concocting. Much to her surprise, the kitchen was empty.

Lexy narrowed her eyes in curiosity. "I wonder why Aurea isn't over there baking? Surely she must have pies to bake for the challenge?"

Cassie craned her neck to look over into the booth. "That is strange. Maybe she's just taking a break."

"Now that we've discovered that Evan Westmore and Amanda Saunders couldn't have been having an affair, that only leaves us with Aurea and Corinne as suspects. At least that I know of..."

"Maybe you can get friendly with that cute Detective Ryan and find out if he has any other suspects. Besides you, I mean."

Lexi felt her stomach clench as she realized *she* was still a suspect. She wondered if Nik Stone and Jake Ryan knew Westmore was gay. If they did, they might eliminate Westmore and Peter Saunders from the suspect list, and that didn't leave too many people. She'd have to work faster to clear herself before their list whittled down to just one suspect - her!

Lexy cut up some ice-cold butter into tiny chunks and put them in the food processor with flour, salt and sugar. She pulsed the mixture until it looked like small crumbles, then added a tiny bit of ice water, alternating pulsing and adding small amounts of water until the dough started to clump together.

Thinking back to her investigation of Westmore's office she remembered the picture of him and the other tuxedo-clad gentleman. With a jolt, she realized the other person must have been his significant other. Lexy kicked herself for not picking up on it at the time.

"I feel so discouraged now that Peter Saunders and Evan Westmore are out of the running in the suspect race." Lexy had spent a lot of time thinking about their motives, and now she felt like she was back to square one. "Although, just because Amanda Scott-Saunders wasn't having an affair didn't mean Peter Saunders didn't kill her."

"True, they did have at least one fight that he admits to and what was with her new clothes, purses, and shoes?   I still say she was up to something." Cassie poured corn syrup and vanilla into a pan with butter and brown sugar. Placing it on the stove, she turned the knob on the gas burner. Lexy heard the tell tale clicking and the poof of gas indicating the burner was on.

Turning the dough out of the food processor, Lexy started rolling it out with a marble rolling pin. Their plan was to make two pies for the contest - a bourbon pecan pie and Lexy's famous coconut cream with a layer of chocolate on the bottom.

"It is kind of strange about Corinne though. How would killing Saunders help her win the contest?" Cassie said as she poured pecans and bourbon into the cooling mixture.

Lexi narrowed her eyes. "You know that's a good question. I don't think eliminating her as a judge would help Corinne, but then again she did win that last contest."

She flipped the dough onto a pie plate and started pinching the edges to even them out along the rim. "Her motivation could be something we don't know about--like maybe Saunders caught her cheating and was going to expose her?"

"Maybe, or maybe she didn't kill Saunders. Maybe she just wanted to mess up your cake so she could win the contest."

"Yeah, but why the warning?"

"Good question." Lexy looked up and thought she saw a familiar figure duck out of sight. "Hey, is that Jake Ryan?"

"That cute detective? Where?" Cassie craned her neck to look around.

"Over there." Lexy pointed in the direction where she thought she had seen him, then shrugged. "Must have been my imagination."

"Ready?" Cassie asked, holding up the pan.

Lexy nodded, then slid the pie plate over for Cassie to pour the mixture in. She looked up again in the direction she had thought she had seen Jake Ryan. She was sure it was him but was perplexed as to why he would duck out of sight. Unless he was watching her. And if he was, that couldn't be a good sign.

Nans looked around the casino, a thrill of excitement running through her. At her age, there weren't many things that made her feel this excited, but covert detective work was one of them. The best part was that no one ever paid much attention to a little old lady, so she was practically invisible. This allowed her to eavesdrop on conversations and follow people virtually undetected.

Back home, the members of the Ladies Detective Club didn't go out much. They mostly investigated cases from the comfort of the retirement center where they lived, using their iPads to do the "leg work" for them. Once in a while, however, they took out Ruth's gigantic late-model Buick to go "in the field" either to follow a suspect or stake out a location. Nans loved doing the field work, and this little task she had taken on for Lexy reminded her of those times.

She rummaged inside her large purse for the Bakery Battles Stadium V.I.P. Pass Lexy had given her. The pass was for guests of the bakers only. She would need it to get inside the stadium, as the general public was not allowed in when there was no competition being taped.

Pulling the large blue-and-white paper from her purse, she clutched it in her hands while she navigated the casino, weaving between banks of slot machines and poker tables.

The clanging of bells and the mechanical spinning of reels was music to her ears and she listened happily while carefully crossing the busy area. A crowd of people cheering on her right caught her attention. Her eyes widened at what she saw.

Aurea Pearce sat at a poker table, the players and bystanders applauding her as she raked in a huge mound of poker chips.

Nans shook her head in disbelief. Aurea was a nasty person and possibly even a murderer; it just didn't seem fair that she should win a big poker pot. *Oh, well, I guess it's true that life isn't fair.*

She continued on to the visitor's entrance of the stadium area. Dutifully showing her pass to the guard at the door, she slipped inside, blending in with the other spectators.

The stadium hummed with activity. Bakers were frantically whipping up pies for the day's challenge. Nans could feel the level of stress - some of the bakers would be eliminated today, so there was a lot riding on creating perfect pies.

Nans breathed in the homey smell of baked pie crust as she made a wide circle around the edge of the stadium. She passed Lexy's booth and caught her eye, giving her a sly wink. The girls were busy at work and she didn't want to interrupt them. Besides, she had work of her own to do.

Making her way around the stadium, she concentrated on using a slow, halting walk. Normally a very fast walker, she had developed a slower pace of walking as part of her surveillance technique because it allowed her to eavesdrop more easily. After all, no one thought twice about an old lady who walked slowly.

She slowed her pace even more in front of Corinne's booth. She noticed Corinne humming while she baked, seemingly enjoying herself despite her dire personal circumstances.

Nans stopped, pretending to admire the pies in the next booth, her ear tuned in Corinne's direction hoping the baker might say something incriminating to her assistant.

A ring tone burst from Corinne's pocket. Looking over out of the corner of her eye, Nans saw the baker pull a cell phone out of her apron and put it to her ear.

She watched Corinne's face grow white, her demeanor darkening.

"I can't talk here." Her voice was barely above a whisper, but Nans had turned up her hearing aid just for the occasion, so she heard it perfectly.

"I'll call you back in a few minutes." Nans looked away as Corinne snapped the phone shut. Then she heard the baker mumble something to her assistant before she rushed out of the booth.

Nans turned in time to see her heading for the hall, then broke out of her slow, halting gait and into a fast walk behind her.

She followed Corinne at a safe pace, then saw her go into the ladies room. After a few seconds, Nans silently opened the door, shutting it slowly so that it didn't make any noise.

The small four-stall bathroom was empty except for Corinne, who was inside one of the stalls. Nans positioned herself at the sink. She could hear Corinne talking on her phone.

"...I told you I'd get it...I have that paper...her out of the way..."

Corinne was talking so low that Nans could only pick out snatches of the conversation despite her cranked-up hearing aid. She leaned in a little closer, feeling a chill run up her spine at the baker's next words.

"I'll do *whatever it takes* to stop the foreclosure."

Nans heard the phone snap shut. She straightened up at the sink, pretending to fix her hair. Corinne came out of the stall and Nans held her breath, hoping the baker wouldn't recognize her. Just as she expected, the other woman barely even glanced her way. *Just another old lady in the casino bathroom.*

Nans slipped out of the bathroom shortly after Corinne. Her sleuthing assignment fulfilled, she turned in the direction of the casino. She had a few hours to kill before Lexy would be done in Bakery Battles Stadium, and she could think of no better place to spend it than at the slot machines.

Chapter Eleven

"I can't believe Aurea tried to push off those half-baked pies on the judges!" Cassie snickered.

Lexy cracked a smile. Not one to laugh at the failures of her competitors she made an exception in this case. "I know. She didn't even start baking them until 20 minutes before time was up. Not sure what she was thinking there, but I can't say I'm sorry. Even her good friend Judge Harvey couldn't save her from that one—at least not without risking her job."

"I think the contest might be down to just you and Corinne, now," Cassie said.

Lexy felt her heart clench. Two days ago she had felt for Corinne and her situation. She even thought the two of them were becoming good friends. But if Corinne had sabotaged her cake and was involved in the murder, then she wanted nothing to do with her.

As she and Cassie got closer to her kitchen, she saw a familiar figure standing there. Jake Ryan. *Was he following her?*

"Hi," she said, her eyebrows raised.

"Hi. I heard you won the pie challenge. Congratulations."

"Thanks...did you come all the way here just to congratulate me?"

Jake smiled, showing off his perfect white teeth and dimples. "Actually, I have some information about one of the suspects you might be interested in."

"Oh, I didn't realize you guys shared information about one of your suspects with another one of your suspects."

Jake glanced around covertly, then lowered his voice. "Well, I'm not supposed to, but this one could help you with the contest too. What do you say? Come over to the bar with me and I'll tell you over a drink."

Was he flirting?

Lexy felt tempted by his puppy-dog look and the information he promised, but a quick look at her cart and kitchen revealed a pile of dirty dishes and bowls. "I'd love to but..." she waved her hand to indicate the mess.

"Oh, you go ahead I'll clean this up and put everything away." Cassie said.

"Are you sure?" Lexy asked.

"Yeah, no worries. Go." Cassie made shooing motions with her hands.

Lexy shrugged. "OK." She turned to Jake. "Shall we?" She tilted her head in the direction of the casino bar.

"After you." Jake stepped to one side to let Lexy walk past.

They walked side by side down the long, wide hallway. Lexy refrained from asking who the information was about and worked at making idle chitchat.

They selected a table in the corner of the empty bar and Jake went to retrieve their drinks - a soda for her and beer for him.

He set her drink in front of her, then took the seat across the table.

"Well? What's this big news?" Lexy tilted her and raised her eyebrows.

Jake took a swig from his beer, then set his arms on the table, leaning in towards Lexy. "We finished looking at the surveillance tapes and we can rule out one of the suspects-Aurea Pearce."

Lexy felt her shoulders sag. "Really? Why?" She hoped her disappointment didn't show on her face-Aurea was one of the few people she didn't like and Lexy would have preferred that the killer be someone she didn't like.

"The casino surveillance tapes show her at the poker tables from 3:31 am to 6 am. That's the timeframe Saunders was killed, so Aurea couldn't have done it." Jake spread his arms, then settled back in his seat.

Lexy swirled her drink, watching the ice cubes chase each other around the glass. She took a sip. She wondered if Jake knew Westmore was gay. If he did, then he knew Westmore and Peter Saunders weren't likely suspects anymore-at least not because Amanda could have been having an affair with Westmore. Aurea had been ruled out, so that only left *her* as the most eligible suspect. *Was that why Jake seemed to be following her?*

She decided to test him. "So, that leaves Westmore and Saunders as your prime suspects?" she asked.

"We have a few others we are looking at too."

Lexy felt the tension in her shoulders relax, relieved he didn't say they had ruled out Westmore and Saunders.

"Corinne Conners?" She decided to add a new suspect just for some extra insurance.

Jake raised an eyebrow. "What about her?"

"When I found the sabotaged cake, there was glitter on the floor and on the handle of the fridge."

Jake shrugged. "So?"

"I don't use glitter, but Corinne did. Her wedding cakes were loaded with it."

Jake sat up straighter. "Why didn't you mention that before?"

Lexy felt a flush of heat creep into her cheeks. "I didn't realize it until today...I was going to mention it to you."

Jake's eyes narrowed. "I'll have to look into that."

"And that's not all." Lexy looked down. She felt guilt lay a heavy hand on her heart, like she was tattling on a friend to save herself. Then she realized it was all true, and if Corinne was the killer, the police should know the details.

She looked up to see Jake staring at her, waiting for her to continue.

"Corinne has bad money problems. Her house is in foreclosure. I don't know how killing Saunders could help her with that, but she definitely has a strong motive to want to win the contest. Come to think of it, Aurea Pearce has money problems too."

"Yes, we found out she has a gambling problem. But since she couldn't have killed Saunders, I don't think that is relevant...unless she was in on it with someone."

"People do strange things when it comes to money, Detective."

"And you, Lexy...do you have money problems?"

"I assume you've done a check on me just like the others, so you know I don't."

Jake nodded. Behind him Lexy could see a figure gesturing wildly through the frosted-glass wall of the bar. She leaned over to the side to get a better look.

Jake turned around to see what she was looking at. "Who is that?"

The frosted glass distorted her view. Narrowing her eyes, she could just make out a short, older woman with blueish-gray hair, carrying a gigantic purse.

"I'm not sure, but I think it's my grandmother."

Lexy watched Nans take a dainty sip of the tea Jake Ryan had persuaded the bartender to make for her before he discreetly made his exit.

"Jake is such a nice young man. You sure do have a way of attracting the cute detectives. I hope you didn't forget about Jack, though." Nans looked at her slyly over the rim of her cup. Jack and Nans had been neighbors and Nans had a big soft spot for him.

"Of course not...I've just been busy." With all the excitement going on, she *had* been neglecting Jack. She made a mental note to call him as soon as she and Nans were done.

"Oh good, dear. You two make a nice couple."

Lexy remembered how Nans had been gesturing wildly outside the bar to catch her attention. "You seemed very anxious to see me; did you want to tell me something?"

Nans leaned in, her eyes gleaming. "My covert surveillance was a big success."

"Do tell."

"I overheard Corinne talking on the phone. She seemed very upset, like she was being threatened. I heard her say something about some piece of paper that seemed important. She also said she'd do *whatever it takes* to stop the foreclosure." Nans sat back in her seat, a gleam of satisfaction in her eye.

"That doesn't sound good," Lexy said. "What paper was she talking about?"

"I have no idea; she just said she had it. It seemed important somehow."

"I'm still not sure how this ties in with the murder and my cake sabotage, but I can understand how desperate she must feel." Lexy felt her heart drop. "It's too bad. I was really starting to like her..."

Nans put her hand over Lexy's. "This doesn't necessarily mean she is the killer, or that she ruined your cake."

Lexy sighed. "But we don't have many other suspects left."

Nans scrunched her forehead and paused. "There's still Peter Saunders. Usually the husband is the first one I suspect. I wonder if the police have found out any more about him?"

"I don't know. Come to think of it, I haven't seen him around." Lexy glanced over at the bar but there was no sign of Saunders.

"And there is one other clue that I think we may be overlooking," Nans said.

"Oh?"

Nans looked around to make sure no one was within hearing range. "The black book you got from Westmore's office."

"That did seem important, but without knowing what it's about, how can we tell if it has anything to do with the murder?"

"We can't, but I think we need to give it due attention."

Lexy sucked in an ice cube from her drink and crunched it. "That's an idea...if only we could figure out more about what the notations in the book actually mean."

Nans nodded. "By the way, I saw Aurea Pearce win big at the poker tables today."

Lexy's eyes went wide. "*That* explains why she was late getting her pies started." *Hopefully she'll keep gambling and make it easier for me to win the competition.*

Nans noisily slurped her tea, then wiped her mouth with a napkin. "Well, if that's all, I must get back to the slots. I'm on a winning streak, you know."

Lexy smiled. "Well, I wouldn't want to keep you from that."

As she watched Nans disappear into the casino, her thoughts turned to the murder. Something nagged at the back of her mind about the little black book. *Just what did those dates and numbers really mean?*

Maybe now that the police would be looking into Corinne's involvement, she should just let it go. If Corinne was the murderer, and the one who had threatened her, the police would take care of it. Her time would be better spent focusing on winning the last challenge in the competition, not running around trying to find a killer.

Except for one thing.

Lexy had a hard time believing that the perky mother of three would commit murder. It didn't add up. Murdering Saunders did nothing to guarantee Corinne would win the contest and get the money. Unless there was more to it than Lexy realized.

Lexy drained her glass, then pushed away from the table. Tomorrow was the last challenge and contest finale for *Bakery Battles*. She needed to get a good night's rest. She'd need all her wits about her in order to create extraordinary cupcakes that would win the challenge and catch the killer all before the end of the contest.

Chapter Twelve

"Well if it isn't my old friend Jack Perillo. How are you doing?" Nik smiled into the phone.

"Good. Long time no see, huh?"

"Yep. Too long." Nik thought fondly back to the days when she and Jack had worked together. They solved a lot of cases and had become close friends but time and geography had wedged theirs way in the middle, as they so often do, and the two detectives hadn't talked in years.

"I hear you have a murder going on at the *Bakery Battles* contest there. Is that why you called?"

"Yes, one of our persons of interest is from your town. I think you probably know her because she's been involved in murder cases there before."

Nik heard a sharp intake of breath from the other side of the phone.

"Let me guess...is it Lexy Baker?"

"Uh-huh. How did you know?"

"Lexy seems to have a way of being around when murders happen."

"Do you think she could be involved?"

Nik heard Jack laugh on the other end. "Lexy? No, she wouldn't hurt a fly. Do you have evidence?"

"Nothing concrete, but she was the one to find the body, and the victim was strangled with her apron. Plus, the victim was a judge for the contest Baker is in and, apparently, didn't judge her favorably."

"That's all circumstantial. I can assure you Lexy didn't do it. You don't have any better leads?"

"We have a few, but we're checking all our angles. How can you be so positive she didn't do it?"

"Because I know Lexy personally."

"So you vouch for her then?" Nik felt her eyes narrowing, wondering *how* well Jack knew Lexy.

"Yeah, she's not your murderer."

"OK, thanks," Nik said, then added, "it was good to talk to you again."

"Same here Nikki. Good luck with your case."

She snapped the phone shut.

Jake looked at her expectantly. "He doesn't think she could be the killer?"

"Nope. Says he knows her personally."

Nik saw Jakes eyes narrow. "Well perhaps his judgment is clouded depending on how personally he knows her. Ms. Baker can be quite persuasive. I can see how she could fool a man into thinking she was innocent."

Nik raised her eyebrows. "Really? Is that what she has done to *you*?"

Jake laughed. "Not me, I'm immune. But she did give us another lead to check out."

"Who?"

"Another baker, Corinne Conners. According to Lexy, there was glitter near the area where she found her sabotaged cake and Corinne Conners's cakes were loaded with glitter."

"Interesting." Nik tapped her lips with the end of her pencil. "Baker could just be telling you that to throw you off track...or to try to implicate the other girl and ruin her chances of winning. Aren't they in the top three to win the grand prize in *Bakery Battles*?"

"Yes, they are. It could be a ruse, but there's only one way to find out."

"Agreed. See if you can have someone round her up and bring her in."

"We've ruled out Peter Saunders as the killer - the tapes show Amanda leaving the room alone that morning, and the electronics verify the door to the room wasn't opened again until after the body was found. He's been screaming holy hell about us finding the killer, so I'd like to speed things up."

Nik leaned back in her adjustable police-issue chair, the old springs squeaking mechanically. "There's one clue we haven't let out to the public. I'm wondering if we can use that to trap the killer."

"The paper?" Jake asked, eyebrows raised.

"Yes. Judging by the way the piece of paper was clutched in Saunders's hand, the killer must have ripped most of it from her after he killed her. The lab reports just came in and the paper is a very expensive and rare stock. We're trying to trace the source of the paper to see if we can find out who the buyer is, but the lab has a huge backload of cases to work on, so that's not going to happen any time soon."

"Something incriminating must have been on that paper. So, you're thinking if the killer thinks we know what it was, he or she will do something drastic."

Nik nodded. "Now all we have to do is dangle the bait. Since you seem to have such a good rapport with Lexy Baker, and she seems to be in the middle of things, you're the logical person to feed it to her."

###

Lexy worked the bowl of lemon filling, whipping it by hand so as to create the perfect texture. Beside her she could see Cassie mixing together the ingredients for the cupcake batter. Both girls worked silently, at breakneck speed.

Lexy was surprised at how refreshed she felt. She had slept well, despite the stress of the murder investigation and the pressure to win the final bakers challenge.

"The lemon cream filling is ready. I'll put it in the fridge until the cupcakes are cooled."

"OK. What's next on the list?" Cassie asked while pouring batter into the individual cupcake pans that had been lined with specialty paper Lexy had splurged on to give her cupcakes an elegant presentation.

Lexy looked down at the handwritten list they had devised the night before. It was a running checklist of the order in which they needed to make the ingredients for the cupcakes, which would be judged in that days challenge. It was crucial that everything go perfectly, since this was the last challenge in *Bakery Battles*.

The overall winner of the contest would be determined by adding up the scores from all the challenges. If they could score high on this one, Lexy stood an excellent chance of winning the entire contest and taking home the $100,000 grand prize.

"Next we need to make the batter for the chocolate-espresso cupcakes, then put together the frostings for both."

"I'll do the batter." Cassie grabbed the necessary ingredients from the pantry. "I see Aurea isn't in her kitchen yet."

Lexy glanced over at the next booth. "Good. The less work she puts into her cupcakes the better for us. Nans told me she saw her winning a big jackpot, so maybe she doesn't care so much about the contest anymore."

Cassie frowned. "I still feel like we need something more to make our cupcakes stand out... even if Aurea does a half-assed job, we still have Corinne to contend with."

"Don't worry. I have a surprise decoration that's sure to win us high points in the aesthetics department." Lexy felt a satisfied smile curl her lips.

Cassie looked at her with interest. "Spill it. What?"

Lexy put her finger up to her lips "Shhh...I don't want anyone to find out or they might steal my idea." She beckoned Cassie over to the refrigerator.

Looking over her shoulder to make sure no one was watching, she opened the large stainless steel door, then bent down to retrieve something from the bottom shelf. Using the door and her body to shield what was in her hand from the rest of the stadium, she pulled out a long, delicate sugar sculpture.

Lexy felt pride well in her chest as she looked at the fragile piece of edible art. It was 4 inches long and consisted of thin pulls of sugar that were swirled and twisted.

"Wow. When did you make that?" Cassie stared at the sculpture wide-eyed.

"Last night. I've been experimenting with sugar sculpture for a few months and I figure this would be a great time to put my skills to the test. I think if we top the cupcakes with these, that's sure to gain us a few points."

Cassie nodded. "You'll get extra for creativity and skill level."

"That's what I'm hoping." Lexy bent down, carefully putting the sculpture back in its place next to the others. "I want to keep them hidden in here. We'll put them on at the very last minute, so no one else will know what we are up to."

"That's gonna be awesome." Cassie held up her closed fist for a knuckle tap.

Walking back to the table, Lexy picked up the list. "OK, I'll do the-"

Her cell phone made buzzing noises in her pocket, interrupting her.

Lexy dug it out and looked at the screen. *Damn, it's Jack.* She realized she had forgotten to call him yesterday.

"It's Jack...I'll have to take it." Feelings of guilt washed over her as she mustered up her most cheerful voice.

"Jack! How are you?"

"Hi Lexy...good. Well, I've been better actually." Lexy's heart sank as she recognized a serious tone in his voice.

"What's the matter?"

"I just got off the phone with Nikki Stone. Do you want to tell me what's really going on out there?"

Lexy's stomach dropped. *What had Stone told him?*

"It's just what I told you before, Jack." She tried to make her voice light, but it came out in a nervous croak.

"Stone seems to think you are somehow involved in the murder. Are you and Nans doing your usual amateur investigating?"

"No...I mean, not really." Her half-baked answer was met with silence on the other end.

"Well we did look into a few things, but only because the police keep asking me questions," she offered.

"Lexy, we've talked about this before. You need to stop meddling and stay out of the way of the police."

Lexy's back stiffened at his words. *Meddling?* She hated it when he referred to her investigative work as meddling. She and Nans had actually been helpful in many of *his* investigations, providing clues that the police hadn't yet discovered. She was about to remind him of that when his exasperated voice continued on.

"It's just that I'm not out there to bail you out if you get into trouble. Remember, Nikki Stone and her team don't know you like I do and there's a murderer on the loose there. I don't want you to get hurt."

Lexy felt a her heart flip-flop at the tender way he said the last sentence.

"I know, it's just that the police don't seem to be able to get people to talk to them and...well...I do kind of want to clear myself as a suspect."

Jack sighed on the other end. "Do you need me to come out there?"

Lexy thought about it. It would be nice to have him by her side, but the contest would be over tonight, and tomorrow she'd be flying home. There was no time for him to come out now.

"No, I'll be back tomorrow night anyway - hopefully this will all be over by then." Trying to turn the subject away from herself, she asked, "How is Sprinkles?"

"She's great...keeps trying to go over into your yard though." Jack's house was behind Lexy's; their backyards abutted each other. Sprinkles was staying at his house while she was gone but apparently wanted to go back to her own yard.

"Aww...that's cute. I hope she doesn't think I'm at home and ignoring her."

"Oh, don't worry, she's getting plenty spoiled at my place. Might not even want to go back to your place when you get back." Jack's voice belied his fondness for the little dog.

"And you...how are you?" Lexy asked.

"Well, I'm not getting spoiled and I'm pretty sure I *am* going to want to go to your place when you get home," Jack said teasingly.

Lexy laughed into the phone. "How is work going?"

"Good. I just wrapped up a case that Ida helped me on."

Lexy remembered Ida saying she was working with Jack. "She must have loved that, what was the case about?"

Lexy wasn't that interested in the case,\; she had too much going on, but she was glad the topic had moved away from *her* and the Bakery Battles murder.

"You know the textile plant on the corner of Main Street?"

"Yes." Lexy picture the old brick mill building in the center of town that was now used to manufacture all kinds of cloth and textiles.

"One of the accountants was found dead - pushed down the old freight elevator shaft. The killer tried to make it look like an accident."

Lexy felt a chill run up her spine, picturing a body at the bottom of the creepy old elevator shaft. "Uh-huh."

"Our investigation revealed he had been pushed," Jack said with obvious pride. "It turns out the general manager had been skimming money off the top for years. The victim found out and was killed for it."

"How did Ida help you with that?" Lexy wondered.

"The killer was keeping a second set of books in the form of cryptic text messages he sent to himself on his cell phone. Ida helped us figure out what the text messages meant."

"A second set of books?" Lexy's eyebrows furrowed together.

"Yeah, sometimes when people are skimming money, they keep two sets of books. One that has the fake transactions to make it look like everything is on the up and up, and one with the real stuff."

Lexy's mind flashed to Evan Westmore's little black book. Ida had said it contained dates and numbers. Large numbers.

"You mean like with different dates and numbers?" she asked.

"Yes, exactly," Jack answered. "But enough about me, how are you doing in the competition?"

Lexy hardly heard the question; her mind was reeling with possibilities. *Had Evan Westmore been keeping two sets of books?* That still didn't make him a murderer, but it sure did make him guilty of something. Maybe Westmore and Corinne were in on it together?

Suddenly Lexy had a whole new perspective on the situation...and a new plan of action was starting to form.

She realized Jack was still waiting for her answer.

"Good. I could actually pull off a win if I can really wow them in this next challenge. Speaking of which, I have to go get these cupcakes ready or I won't be winning anything at all."

"OK. Well, good luck. Call me tonight and let me know," Jack said.

"Will do."

She hung up the phone feeling a little guilty that she had given him the brush-off. While it was true that she *did* need to tend to the cupcakes, she also had something else in mind.

The conversation about two sets of books had given her an idea. With the cops taking care of questioning Corinne, she needed to get to Westmore's office again - and this time, she had a better idea of where to look.

Chapter Thirteen

Lexy shoved the phone back in her pocket and turned to Cassie. "I think we might have an interesting turn in the murder case."

Cassie looked up, her body straightening, head cocked to one side. "From Jack?"

"Indirectly. Something he said."

Cassie had stopped in the middle of icing a batch of cupcakes. She stared at Lexy with furrowed brows, her frosting-coated spatula high in the air.

Lexy stepped closer to Cassie, dropping her voice to a whisper. "I need to take another look in Westmore's office. In a few hours, he'll be doing the filming for the lead-in to the cupcake judging challenge. That will be the perfect time."

"Lexy, that sounds dangerous..."

"I'll be careful. I just need a few minutes and I think I know exactly where to look."

"But what are you looking for?" Cassie asked.

Out of the corner of her eye, Lexy saw Jake Ryan approaching their booth.

"I'll tell you later," she said, angling her head in his direction.

They both watched Jake saunter toward them, his charming smile lighting his face.

"Ladies, how goes the cupcake baking?" He craned his head to look at the cupcakes Cassie was frosting.

"Good. We're presenting two cupcake recipes that are really popular in our bakery back home. I think we are going to do really well."

"I think you lost one of your competitors." He nodded toward Aurea Pearce's empty booth. "She packed up her bags and left in the middle of the night."

"She did?" Lexy looked sideways into Aurea's booth with narrowed eyes. "Why would she do that?"

"Rumor has it she owed a lot of money to people who are pretty insistent on getting it back on time. I think she might have been afraid they would catch up with her."

"Oh, well she fell pretty far behind in the last challenge, so she wasn't much competition anyway."

"Right, Corinne is your big competition now, I hear. We're pulling her in for questioning momentarily."

Lexy felt her heart clench. Jake was looking at her as if he thought she had mentioned the other baker on purpose, to increase her odds of winning.

"What about Peter Saunders?" Lexy still harbored hope that Corinne was innocent and that someone else had murdered the judge.

"He's been cleared. Records show he was in his room when his wife was murdered," Jake said. He turned his attention back to the cupcakes Cassie was working on. Tilting his head, he walked closer bending down for a better look.

"These cupcake papers - they're very nice. I haven't seen these before."

Lexy felt her heart swell with pride. "Those are specialty papers I ordered for the contest. I wanted to make my cupcakes stand out."

"It's funny you mention specialty paper. Amanda Scott-Saunders had a piece of specialty paper clutched in her hand when she was murdered. It looked as if the murderer had ripped it out after she was killed."

Lexy gasped, her eyes growing wide. She remembered Nans saying how Corinne had mentioned something about a paper. Maybe Corinne really was the murderer, but if she was, where did Westmore fit in? Could they have been in on it together? Or maybe he wasn't even involved at all.

"Is something wrong?" Jake was looking at her intently.

"N-no," she stammered. *Should she tell him about the conversation Nans had overheard?*

Jake turned his attention back to her cupcakes. "Can I have one of these cupcake papers?"

Lexy's mouth fell open. "Surely you don't think..."

Jake smiled, touching her arm lightly. "Of course not...well, it is one more clue that points in your direction," he teased.

Lexy felt her cheeks grow red as a flush of anger swept her body. She jerked her arm away. Stomping over to her supply rack, she grabbed a paper cupcake holder and thrust it out toward him.

"Here, take it."

"Lexy, don't be mad. I can compare a sample and rule you out." The puppy-dog look on Jakes face as he reached for the cupcake paper did nothing to soften her anger.

"I understand," she said sharply. "Now, if you don't mind, I have to finish baking these cupcakes...that is, if I'm not under arrest."

"Of course not. Thanks." He held up the paper, then turned and walked away.

She glared at his retreating back for a few seconds before returning to her work.

"Sheesh, I don't know what to make of him," Cassie said.

"Me neither. He acts friendly, but I get the impression he is watching me-waiting for me to trip up."

"That was interesting, what he said about the paper."

"It sure was. I kept thinking about how Nans heard Corinne say she had the paper. Nans seemed to think that paper was very important."

"Maybe Corinne murdered Saunders to get the paper--whatever it is." Cassie offered.

Lexy nodded. She was thinking the same exact thing. But if that were true, where did that leave Westmore?

Lexy shifted into high gear. "We better speed up the cooking. I want to be done in plenty of time to get to Westmore's office. I have a feeling the answers to some of our questions are in his locked filing cabinet."

###

Nik hurried down the plain tiled hallway of the police station towards Interrogation Room 3. Jake fell in beside her, rushing to keep up.

"Did you let a hint drop to Lexy about the paper?" Nik asked.

Jake nodded. "I could tell by her reaction that it hit a nerve. She tried to pretend like it didn't, but she knows something. Funny thing is, she was using some specialty cupcake papers for her contest entry."

Nik stopped, turning to Jake. "Do you think it's the same paper?"

"Her papers were colored and the one in the victims hand was off-white. I took a sample and handed it off to the lab for a comparison."

"Good. Keep Styles and McManus on her. I want to know where she goes and what she does." Nik continued on toward the interrogation room. Peeking through the window in the doorway she could see Corinne Conners sitting at the table, her white-knuckled hands clasped tightly in front of her.

Nik opened the door, sweeping into the room with Jake in tow.

"Ms. Conners." She nodded at Corinne.

Corinne looked up, her wide eyes darting between Nik and Jake.

"I don't understand why I'm here."

Nik heard Corinne's voice tremble and wondered if it was because she really was uncertain as to why she was there or whether she was afraid they had discovered she was the murderer.

"We have some questions regarding an incident in Bakery Battles Stadium that we think may be related to the murder of Amanda Scott-Saunders." Nik's eyes narrowed as she watched Corinne's reaction.

"What's that got to do with me? I wasn't involved in any incident," Corinne said blinking rapidly.

Nik opened a manila folder, producing an enlarged copy of the picture of the sabotaged cake Lexy had sent to Jake. She slid it across the table to Corinne. "Recognize this?"

Corinne's brow furrowed. "No."

"Someone did this to Lexy Baker's wedding cake for the wedding challenge competition. Someone clearly wanted to either cause her to lose the contest or back off from looking into the murder."

Corinne gasped. "You think *I* did that?"

"You won the challenge, didn't you?"

"I won that contest fair and square! I would never ruin someone else's cake to win a challenge." Corinne's eyes were blazing, her chin high in the air.

Nik leaned across the table. "Well, then maybe you can explain why we found glitter around the sabotaged cake - the same glitter that was on the cake you won the contest with."

Corinne's face crumbled. Covering her face with her hands, she burst into tears.

"I..only...wanted...to look...at it." She wrenched out the words between sobs.

"So you *were* there." Nik sat back in her chair.

"Yes, but I only wanted to *look* at her cake to see what I was up against. I didn't do *that* to it." Corinne jabbed her finger at the picture of the cake.

Nik cocked an eyebrow at Jake. *Could she be telling the truth?*

"So the cake looked fine when you saw it?"

Corinne sniffed, wiping her eyes. "Yes. I only wanted to sneak a peeak at the competition. I know it was wrong, but I swear I didn't ruin Lexy's cake!"

"What time were you in the kitchen?"

Corinne bit the inside of her cheek. "I'm not sure...I think it was around seven."

"Did you see anyone else?"

"Yes!" Corinne brightened. "As I was leaving, I saw Evan Westmore coming down the aisle. When he saw me, he kind of hesitated, but then I gave him a little wave and turned off onto a side aisle."

Nik exchanged a look with Jake.

Corinne's eyes narrowed. "You don't think Westmore would have done it, do you?"

"Well, he didn't have a cake in the competition, so if he did, I can only think of one reason why he would have," Jake said.

Nik looked at Jake nodding her head towards the door.

"Excuse us for a minute, Ms. Conners."

Corinne nodded, watching the two detectives exit the room.

Nik leaned her shoulder against the door and looked back in at Corinne. "Do you think she's telling the truth?"

Jake rubbed his forehead. "I don't know. We did see Westmore going in there that night on the video, so she *is* telling the truth about that part."

A noise at the end of the hall caught their attention. Nik and Jake turned to see the short, stocky Detective Morse standing with a sheet of paper in his hand.

"Detective Stone. I have the lab report back on the paper. And the report on the paper you sent in too Detective Ryan."

Nik raised her eyebrows. "Was the cupcake paper a match?"

"No. Similar stock but not a match."

"So that rules out the paper being one of Lexy Bakers cupcake liners, but it doesn't necessarily rule Baker out as the murderer," Jake said.

"Were you able to find out where the paper was purchased?" Nik asked.

"Yep, and also who purchased it."

Nik and Jake exchanged an excited look. "Who?" they said in unison.

"It was purchased online from a custom paper supply in New York about a week ago-by Evan Westmore," Morse said.

"Westmore," Nik said biting her cheek. "Wait a minute...I think I might have an idea of what's going on now."

She started down the hall, then, turning back, she barked, "Morse - you let Corinne Conners go. Ryan, follow me. We have a few things to check out about Evan Westmore and the *Bakery Battles* competition."

Chapter Fourteen

Lexy fidgeted with the spatula, keeping one eye on the clock. It was almost time for the taping to begin, which meant she would have only a few minutes to get into Westmore's office.

"You're sure you'll be able to finish this stuff up?" she asked Cassie for what seemed like the twentieth time.

"Sure, there's not much left. If you don't get back by the time I see the judges come around, I'll put the sugar sculptures on top and make an excuse for you."

"OK, I think it's time for me to go." Lexy felt her stomach roll as she stood up.

"Good luck," Cassie whispered.

Lexy squinted, looking down the long aisle toward the back of the stadium where she could see the crew setting up the cameras for the initial taping. Satisfying herself that Westmore was among them, she turned, hurrying in the direction of his office.

Slipping inside, she crossed to the filing cabinet. It had been locked when she had come here at night. She crossed her fingers, hoping Westmore kept it unlocked during the daytime hours. Her heart pounded in her ears as she took the little black book from her back pocket.

Holding her breath, she tried the top drawer. It slid open and she let her breath out in a big whoosh.

Now if she only knew what she was looking for.

Lexy rifled through the folders trying to find anything that looked like an accounting ledger. She wanted to compare what was on the actual ledgers to the few entries from the black book that Ida had deciphered for her.

The first drawer didn't have what she was looking for. She moved to the second. Inside, an accounting ledger caught her eye. She pulled it out. Running her fingers down the side, she looked for a matching date. *Bingo!* Comparing the numbers next to the date in the ledger with the numbers in the black book, she could see they were different. Surely that must mean-

Her thoughts were interrupted by a noise in the hall. She shoved the ledger back in the drawer, rammed the drawer shut, and spun around just in time to see the doorknob turning.

Lexy felt her legs go weak as she watched the door open. Evan Westmore stepped into the room. She watched his mouth drop open and his eyes go wide when he noticed her standing there.

They stared at each other in stunned silence for a long second.

"What are you doing here?" he demanded.

Lexy felt dizzy, her mind spinning to come up with an excuse for her presence in his office.

"Someone said I could find the challenge enrollment forms in here." She blurted out the first thing she could think of.

Westmore's eyes narrowed. "Who said that?"

He took a step toward her. She shuffled sideways around the desk, holding the black book behind her.

"O-one of the other bakers," she stuttered.

Westmore looked at the filing cabinet she had been leaning her back against.

"Did you find them?" He moved toward her again and she backed farther behind the desk.

"N-no."

"What do you have behind your back?"

Lexy felt a jolt of electricity pierce her heart. She slipped the black book into her back pocket. "Nothing." She spread her hands at her sides.

Westmore's eyes narrowed. "You've been checking up on me, haven't you?"

"No," Lexy lied. Looking down at the desk, her eyes caught the notepaper she had noticed on her previous trip to his office. Suddenly she remembered Jake telling her about the expensive paper that was clutched in Saunders's hand...

specialty paper just like the notepaper she was looking at.

Lexy felt everything click in place like the pieces of a puzzle. The book with coded numbers and dates, the expensive items in Westmore's office, the expensive clothing Saunders had been buying, the specialty paper. Westmore and Saunders weren't lovers - they were pulling some sort of embezzlement scam on the Bakery Battles contest.

Lexy felt a jolt of panic - Westmore *was* the murder. She knew she had to get away, but her legs felt like lead.

She edged around the desk toward the door, praying the look on her face didn't give away the fact that she had figured out what Westmore had done.

Westmore moved between her and the door. The twisted grimace on his face and evil gleam in his eyes made her stomach plummet - Westmore already knew she had figured it out.

Nik reached across her desk to grab the manila folder filled with information they had gathered on Westmore. She pursed her lips, leafing through the papers.

"See if you can get a list of Westmore's purchases and bank account transactions," she said without looking up.

"And hurry," she called after Jake as he ran off to do her bidding.

Nik stared out the window, her mind racing. Westmore had a shady past. He was in the stadium when Saunders was murdered, but so were a lot of other people. Corinne claimed to have seen him the night the cake was sabotaged. Most importantly, Amanda Scott-Saunders had been clutching a piece of paper Westmore had purchased at the time of her death.

She tapped her fingernails impatiently on the desk. *Where was Ryan with that bank account report?* If her theory proved true, then it was a safe bet Westmore was the killer, and she didn't want to waste any time bringing him in.

Out of the corner of her eye she saw Jake rushing across the squad room, a long piece of paper in his hand. She stood to greet him.

"Check this out. He's made some pretty big deposits over the past few weeks." Jake shoved the paper in front of her.

Nik scanned the bank account summary. "He certainly has - much more than his salary would account for. This proves my theory. Westmore was embezzling money from the *Bakery Battles* competition."

"But why kill Saunders?" Jake asked.

Nik bit he inside of her cheek. "Well, we don't have any proof that he *did* kill her. But my gut instinct says he did. Maybe she was in on it with him and he wanted to get her out of the way so he could have all the money, or maybe she caught him at it."

"What about Conners and Baker?"

"Hard to tell how many people were involved... speaking of Baker, have Styles and McManus checked in yet?"

As if on cue, the small two-way radio attached to Jake's belt squawked. "Ryan, you there?" A distorted voice sounded from the radio.

Jake plucked it from his belt, pressing the button on the side. "Yep."

"The subject is on the move. Went to Westmore's office about five minutes ago. Several minutes later Westmore met her there."

Nik felt her heart freeze. She looked at Jake.

"A rendezvous? Maybe Ms. Baker *was* in on it with Westmore - they could have been fixing the contest for her to win. Maybe *they* framed Corinne Conners to get her disqualified and chased Pearce off," Jake said.

"It could be that, or Ms. Baker could be doing some amateur sleuthing, which could prove to be fatal. Either way, we better get to Westmore's office pronto. Have Styles and McManus meet us there."

Nik grabbed two bullet-proof vests from the hooks on the wall and tossed one to Jake. Shrugging her arms through the vest, she watched Jake wrestle with his while issuing the order to the other detectives through the two-way radio. Then she grabbed her gun and ran to the car. Jake jumped in beside her and they sped off, sirens blaring, toward Bakery Battles Stadium.

Lexy felt dizzy. She grabbed the edge of the desk for stability. *She had to stall Westmore - keep him talking until she could figure out how to get past him to the door.*

"I had a feeling you were on to me. Too bad you didn't heed my warning," Westmore sneered, taking a step toward her.

"Warning?"

"The cake. I tried to warn you off, but you couldn't stop meddling, could you?"

Meddling? There was that word again. Lexy straightened her back, her cheeks growing pink with anger.

"You ruined my cake?"

Westmore laughed. "Too bad it didn't get you kicked out of the competition...but you won't be in it much longer anyway."

Lexy kept her eyes on Westmore, feeling along the desk for something sharp. *Where was a good old-fashioned letter opener when you needed one?*

"But why?" Lexy could feel the twitch in her eye start up and squeezed her eyes shut to try to stop it. When she opened them, Westmore was almost beside her.

"You were getting too close to the truth. It could ruin me and I can't let that happen."

"Truth?" *Maybe if she played dumb he'd let her go.*

"Don't play dumb. I know you took my black book. The one with my second set of numbers. In fact, I bet that's what you are hiding behind your back." He lunged forward. Grabbing her arm roughly, he shoved his hand into her back pocket and pulled out the book.

"I knew it!" He seemed almost gleeful.

"So you were embezzling money?" Lexy tried to twist her arm free, but Westmore was surprisingly strong for a wimpy-looking guy.

"That's right."

"And Saunders was in on it with you...you killed her so you could have all the money to yourself."

Westmore laughed. "That bitch. She wasn't in on it; she was blackmailing me! Demanding money every week. She was bleeding me dry. That morning, I met her with a payoff. She was so smug...I just couldn't let her continue. I handed her the money, but when she turned to leave, I grabbed an apron from the hook and choked the life out of her. Then I took my envelope of money from her, shoved her body under the shelving, turned down the thermostat, and left."

Lexy's eyes went wide. *The scrap of paper in Saunders's hand was from an envelope, not a piece of paper.*

"That's why it was so cold in the freezer; you knew the body wouldn't smell," she said.

Westmore sneered.

"But why did you use *my* apron to kill her?"

"That was just coincidence. I merely grabbed the closest one. Of course, I had no idea it would cause you to continuously stick your nose in where it doesn't belong." Westmore tightened his grip on her arm. His eyes looked past her at something on the wall. "If it wasn't for your meddling, the body might not have been discovered until the contest was over. And now, unfortunately, I'm going to have to kill you, too."

He reached past her grabbing a necktie hanging on the wall. Lexy pulled back and kicked out. She heard him grunt as her steel toed stilettos connected with his shin. His grip loosened enough for her to wriggle away. She turned to run.

Pain exploded in her head as he grabbed her pony-tail, yanking her back toward him and leaving her neck exposed. He threw the tie around her neck, wrapped both ends tightly in his hands, and pulled.

Lexy felt like her esophagus was being crushed. She clutched at the fabric around her neck, her vision going gray around the edges. She heard a big bang just as she was beginning to black out and wondered if that was what death sounded like.

"Let go of her, Westmore!"

Lexy figured she must have gone to hell when she heard the voice of Detective Nik Stone blaring in her ears. She felt the tightness loosen around her neck as she dropped to the floor. She inhaled a big gulp of air and opened her eyes.

The room had burst into a hive of activity. Nik Stone had Westmore up against the wall. Two police officers were inspecting the office. Jake Ryan scrambled to her side.

"Are you OK?" he asked.

Lexy's hands went to her raw, bruised throat. "I...think...so." The words came out in a croak.

Jake helped her up as they watched Nik roughly handcuff Westmore and hand him over to Styles and McManus, who escorted him out the door.

Lexy felt a quiver of fear as Stone fixed her with an angry glare. "You're OK?"

Lexy nodded.

"What did you think you were doing, coming in here?" Stone demanded.

Lexy swallowed. "I suspected Westmore was embezzling money." She pointed to the black book on the top of the desk. "That book has coded transactions...a second set of books for accounting."

Nik raised an eyebrow. "And you thought you would come here and catch him all by yourself?"

Lexy felt her cheeks burn. It did sound kind of stupid now that she thought about it. "I just

141

wanted to find more proof to show you. I thought I could compare the ledgers in the filing cabinet and find out for sure."

Nik sighed. "Well you did do one thing for us. You let us catch him in the act of trying to kill you."

"How did you guys know I was in here?" Lexy wrinkled her brow, marveling at the precise timing. A few minutes later and she would have been a goner.

"We had Styles and McManus following you, but we might not have been here if Conners didn't raise my suspicions by telling me that she saw Westmore the night your cake was sabotaged."

Lexy felt her eyes grow wide. "So Corinne had nothing to do with this?"

Nik shook her head. "We don't think so."

Lexy looked at her watch. "Oh, no, the contest! I have to get back-the cupcake challenge has already started!"

Lexy shook off Jake's hand which was still resting on her arm and bolted out of the room. As she ran down the hall she could hear Nik yelling after her: "Wait! We still have some questions for you!"

Chapter Fifteen

Lexy skidded to a stop beside Cassie just as she was about to place the sugar sculptures on top of the first batch of cupcakes.

"Wait...don't put those on."

Cassie turned in Lexy's direction, her brow wrinkled. "What?"

"Just put them out without the sculptures. The judges are only two booths down."

"I think we still have time-"

"No," Lexy cut her off, "let's just get them on the stands and out to the table."

Cassie shrugged and turned her attention to stacking the cupcakes neatly on the tiered stands they had bought especially for the cupcake presentation.

"Did you find what you wanted at Westmore's office?" Cassie asked.

"And then some. Westmore caught me in the act and tried to kill me! The detectives showed up just in time and arrested him. Lexy whispered sharply, her hand going to her throat.

Cassie spun to face her, concern flooding her blue eyes. "What? Your neck is bruised! Are you OK?"

Lexy nodded, "I'm ok. Detective Stone saved the day just in time, but the important thing is Westmore admitted to being the murderer. He's also the one who ruined our cake."

Cassies eyes went wide. "Why did he kill Amanda?"

Lexy lowered her voice. "She caught him embezzling money from the contest and was blackmailing him."

"Holy crap." Cassie opened her mouth to say more but was interrupted by the judges appearing at their booth.

"Your cupcakes make a lovely presentation with the paper and the stand," Judge Lutner said. Lexy felt her heart warm as the others nodded their approval.

"The cupcakes themselves are nice but perhaps a little plain," Grace Harvey said.

Lexy watched the head judge Tim Gartner purse his lips while he looked the cupcakes up and down, then jotted notes on his notepad.

Finally the judges smiled, nodded, and moved on.

Lexy felt like she had been holding her breath the whole time.

"Looks like we did OK," Lexy said.

Cassie shrugged. "Judge Harvey did say they were plain. Those sugar sculptures would have jazzed them up."

Lexy glanced back wistfully at the refrigerator where the sculptures were. They *would* have improved the appearance, most likely giving her high points for aesthetics, but Lexy had her reasons for leaving them off.

"Well, hopefully we will make up for it in the tasting portion of the challenge."

"If we make it that far."

Cassie leaned her head toward Lexy. "Tell me more about Westmore...what happened in there?"

Lexy explained how she had gone to the office and found the ledger, only to be surprised by Westmore, who admitted to killing Saunders before he tried to kill her.

"I hate to admit it, but Nik Stone saved my life," Lexy said.

"Lucky thing. Maybe Jack is right about not getting involved in these investigations." Cassie raised a pierced eyebrow at Lexy.

Lexy felt her cheeks flush but was saved from further admonitions by the sight of Tim Gartner heading toward their booth.

"You've made it to the tasting round, so please bring your cupcakes over," he said.

Lexy and Cassie sprang into action, loading the cupcake displays onto a stainless steel cart, which they wheeled across the stadium to the taste judging area.

On the other side of the stadium, Lexy was pleased to see that Corinne was one of the contestants who had made it to the tasting round. Lexy wheeled her cart over and took her place in between Corinne and another baker she had only met fleetingly. Corinne cast a worried glance in Lexy's direction, but Lexy smiled at her reassuringly.

Lexy shuffled her feet nervously as she watched the judges take their places at the table across from them. The area behind them was filled with various spectators. The camera crew was already recording the activities.

Lexy watched Tim Gartner take the podium, marveling at how quickly the contest had adjusted after the excitement of Westmore's arrest.

As Gartner made the usual introductions, Lexy's thoughts turned to Westmore. Her hand went to her throat; the skin felt raw and she rubbed it uneasily. She felt her stomach churn as she realized how close to death she had come. Maybe Jack *was* right...maybe she should stop meddling in murders. She hated to admit it, but it was becoming somewhat of a fun hobby and she loved working with Nans and the Ladies Detective Club. Perhaps she would just try to be more careful in the future.

"...wonderfully light lemon filling." The words took Lexy out of her thoughts and she smiled at the judge's compliment.

"The taste combination is perfect and your chocolate espresso is rich and moist - one of the best cupcakes I have tasted today," Judge Harvey said.

Lexy smiled and nodded. "Thank you."

With a start, she realized she hadn't even paid attention to what the judges had said about the other contestants' cupcakes-she had been too lost in her own thoughts.

Gartner stepped to the podium, the scorecard in his hand. Lexy felt her mouth go dry realizing they were about to announce the winner of this challenge.

"The judges have scored each cupcake on aesthetics and taste." He waved the cards in the air. "I have the results here and am happy to announce the third-place ribbon. With 3 points for aesthetics and four points for taste, the ribbon goes to..."

Lexy bit her bottom lip as he paused dramatically.

"Marg Rupert." Lexy heard a burst of applause as the baker went up to collect her ribbon. Since this was the last challenge, there were only three finalists, so that left Lexy and Corinne in the running for first place. She glanced sideways at Corinne, who was fidgeting behind her cart of cupcakes.

"Lexy, Corinne." Tim nodded at each of them in turn. "It was a tough decision between the two of you. In the end, one of you won by a hair with a better presentation."

Another dramatic pause jangled Lexy's nerves.

"The second-place ribbon, goes to the baker who won 5 points for taste and 4 points for aesthetics: Lexy Baker! Which means Corinne Conners is the winner with 5 points for both taste and aesthetics!"

Lexy swelled with pride as she and Corinne went to the podium to accept their ribbons. She should have been disappointed she lost by a small margin, but in reality she was happy the other woman won. She felt her heart grow when she saw the smile on Corinne's face, which was flushed with excitement, and she knew she had made the right decision. But when Corinne glanced over at Lexy, her smile faded.

"Congratulations ladies," Tim said, as Lexy and Corinne made their way back to stand behind their carts.

"As you know, this is the last challenge in *Bakery Battles*. We will now pick the overall winner by adding up the scores from all the challenges. The baker with the highest score will win the grand prize of $100,000 and a spread in *American Baker Magazine*."

Everyone applauded loudly, including Lexy and Corinne.

"There is also a generous second prize of $20,000 and a third prize of $2000. We will break for an hour and then announce the winners right here."

Tim stepped down from the podium. The camera crew stopped filming and the crowd started to break up. Everyone would take a short break and return in an hour to hear the final judging.

Lexy saw Corinne turning to leave and called after her.

"Corinne, wait up!"

Corinne turned stiffly to face her and Lexy's heart dropped when she saw the stricken look on her face. She forced herself to walk over to the other baker - she had some unfinished business that needed to be taken care of before the final winner was announced.

"Congratulations!" Lexy said, opening her arms to hug the other baker. She saw that Corinne was near tears. Corinne covered her face as Lexy put her arms around her.

"Oh, Lexy, I'm so sorry."

"Why?" Lexy asked.

"I didn't mean to cheat...I only wanted to peek at your wedding cake," Corinne said through tears.

"Oh, that? Don't be silly. You didn't see anything I was trying to keep secret anyway."

Lexy's heart lifted when she saw Corinne's face brighten.

"Really?"

Lexy nodded.

"So you're not mad?"

"No, not at all."

"Oh, thank you!" Corinne returned Lexy's hug, a big smile on her face, the blue ribbon clutched in her hand.

"I was afraid you would be mad at me. When the police questioned me about it, they thought I ruined your cake. I swear I didn't touch it!"

"I know. Westmore did it. He confessed to me," Lexy said.

Corinne's eyes opened wide. "I saw him that night. He was walking toward your booth. But why?" She looked around. "Come to think of it, where *is* Westmore?"

Lexy explained the whole story to Corinne, who listened wide-eyed.

"Wow. I had no idea." Corrinne looked around. "Hey, I have to go freshen up to get ready for the final announcement." She shook her hands out. "I'm so nervous!"

"Me too! I think we both have a good chance. Good luck!" Lexy said, genuinely meaning it.

"Good luck to you too," Corinne said, giving Lexy a quick hug.

They walked off in opposite directions. Lexy felt like bats were flying around in her stomach. In less than an hour, the whole contest would be over and one of the bakers would be $100,000 richer with a great opportunity ahead of them.

Lexy wanted to win, but she was also rooting for Corinne. The other baker needed the money a lot more than she did, plus she had three young kids to support.

Lexy smiled to herself, certain she had made the right decision, as she sped off to her room to freshen up and then gather Nans and Cassie for the final announcement.

Lexy took in a deep breath and eyed the entrance to Bakery Battles Stadium for what would probably be the last time. In a few minutes, the winner would be announced, the kitchens would be packed up, and everyone would be on their way home and back to their normal lives.

"Good luck, dear." Nans gave her a hug.

Cassie held out her fist for a knuckle tap. "Good luck!"

"Thanks." Lexy smiled, her stomach rolling over like a cement mixer and feeling just as heavy.

She broke off from Nans and Cassie to go to the far side of the stadium where a special section was setup for all the bakers. In the preliminary finals, there would be no taping, and the majority of the bakers would be eliminated. Only the seven bakers with the most points would continue on to the taped finale. Nans and Cassie would be waiting in the spectator stands.

Lexy scanned the crowd. Locating Corinne over in the corner, she waved a greeting and proceeded to make her way over just as Tim Gartner started to address the crowd of bakers.

"First of all, on behalf of *Bakery Battles*, I'd like to thank all of you. As you know, the contest has had its challenges this year."

A murmur went through the crowd, and Lexy could see many of the bakers nodding.

"The baking has been top-notch and you've all done such a wonderful job that it's been hard to choose the finalists," he continued. "But, only one baker can win and it is time to narrow down the group to the top seven who will go on to the grand finale."

Tim held up a piece of paper. "This card has the names of those lucky seven bakers. I'm going to read them off. If you are one of them, step over here to the right. Everyone else can start packing up their kitchens. Thank you for participating in *Bakery Battles* and good luck."

Lexy clenched her hands into fists, her shoulders tense. She *thought* she had done well enough to make it into the top seven, but she still felt anxious to hear her name.

The room fell silent, all the bakers holding their breath as Tim read the names.

"Rudy Abru, Hanna Anderson, Jason Bach, Lexy Baker, Corinne Conners, Mandy Hudson, Bill Salida. Congratulations - you've made it into the top seven!"

Lexy let her breath out in a big whoosh and clapped with the rest of the bakers. *She made it!*

She joined the other six bakers on the right. Amidst high fives and hugs, they watched the remaining bakers file out.

"If you are all set, we can go into the other area now. The camera crews are ready to start taping. Congratulations to all of you - you did a fine job." Tim made the rounds, shaking hands with each of them, then they followed him out into the other room where the camera crews and spectators were waiting.

Lexy took her place in line with the other bakers facing the judges. She could feel her pulse beating in her neck: her throat dried up and her hands got clammy. *Could this really be the final judging for Bakery Battles?* It seemed surreal to think that in a few minutes one of them would have an extra $100,000 and a magazine opportunity.

Tim walked to the podium. The cameras started to roll. Lexy listened while he announced that the final judging was taking place and then said a little bit about each judge and how the entries were judged on taste and appearance with the scores from all the challenges being tallied up to produce the grand-prize winner.

"I'd like to add, that *Bakery Battles* has been proud to host the finest bakers in America." He waved his card at the group of bakers. Lexy smiled and nodded with the rest of them. "I'd like to give all of them the grand prize, but of course, only one can win."

"First, I'd like to announce the four runners-up. Each will receive $250 worth of equipment for their kitchens from our sponsor, the Bakery Connection. They are...Rudy Abru, Hanna Anderson, Jason Bach, and Mandy Hudson!"

Lexy felt relief and excitement. *She was in the top three!*

The clapping died down and Tim continued on. "For the third-place prize, including a check for $2,000, please congratulate...Bill Salida!"

Lexy's heart hammered in her chest; her knees felt weak. That left only her and Corinne-one of them was the grand-prize winner and the other the second-prize winner.

"Lexy...Corinne...You've both been great competitors. Your scores were pretty close, but one of you will be the grand-prize winner of $100,000 and a spread in *American Baker Magazine*. The other will get a nice prize too - a check for $20,000."

The spectators clapped enthusiastically. Lexy forced herself to breathe - either way she was going home with a big, fat check.

"And the grand-prize winner is..."

Tim paused. Lexy held her breath, feeling dizzy with anticipation. She figured if she was watching this on television, she'd be subjected to a series of commercials before she could find out who the winner was. She was grateful she didn't have to wait 5 minutes in real life.

"Corinne Conners!"

Lexy let out her breath in a whoosh of air. She turned to see Corinne jumping up and down. Confetti rained down from the ceiling as she embraced her friend.

"Congratulations! The prize couldn't go to a more deserving baker." Lexy meant every word of it. She released Corinne and watched her walk up to the podium to pose for the cameras with an oversized version of the $100,000 check.

Lexy smiled as she turned away scanning the crowd for Nans and Cassie. She spotted them in the corner, waved, and headed over to them.

"Congratulations!" Nans said. "I think you should have won first prize, but you still did pretty good."

Lexy nodded.

"Nice work!" Cassie said.

"I couldn't have done it without you." Lexy smiled at her friend.

"There's one thing I just can't figure out." Cassie narrowed her eyes at Lexy.

"What's that?"

"Why didn't you want to put the sugar sculptures on the cupcakes? I think we would have won first prize with those extra points."

Lexy shrugged, glancing over at Corinne with a smile.

"Hey, wait a minute." Cassie's eyes got bigger. "Lexy...you did it on purpose, didn't you?"

Lexy blushed, looking away. It was true, they might have won the contest, but Lexy was happy with the $20,000 and even happier knowing the big prize would go to a family who really needed the money to start over.

She hooked her arms through Cassie's and Nans'. "Sometimes winning isn't about getting the biggest prize. Now, let's go pack up the kitchen, collect our check, and go home."

Epilogue

Lexy looked down her straw at the red liquid swirling between ice cubes in the gigantic skull-shaped glass mug sitting on the table in front of her. She took a long sip.

Leaning back in her chair, she looked around the crowded outdoor bar at the Treasure Island hotel. With regret, she realized this was the first time she'd had a chance to actually enjoy her trip to Vegas. Too bad it would be short-lived. She was only killing time in the bar before their limo arrived to take them to the airport.

She breathed in the dry twilight desert air. Across the table, Detective Nik Stone raised her delicate martini glass.

"A toast to my favorite amateur sleuths." She tipped her glass toward Nans and then Lexy.

Lexy, Cassie, Nans, and Jake brought up their glasses to clink with Nik's.

"I still can't believe you guys used me to do the dirty work." Lexy glared at Jake.

"Well, not *all* the work. But we did find you useful," he said.

"Come on, admit it, you wouldn't have stopped looking no matter what. We just made good use of your efforts. *And* kept an eye on you so you didn't get into trouble," Nik said. "Speaking of which, you really shouldn't make a habit of getting involved in these investigations, Lexy - it *can* be very dangerous."

Lexy rolled her eyes. Nik was starting to sound like Jack - did all detectives talk like that? She couldn't help but smile, thinking she'd be home with Jack-and Sprinkles soon.

"You know," said Cassie, "there's still a couple of strange things about the case that I don't get. Like what really happened to Aurea Pearce?"

"And what was the paper I heard Corinne talking about?" Nans added.

"We got word Aurea took off in a hurry. She owed a lot of money to a lot of different people. People you don't want to owe money to. When she had a big win at the poker tables, she fled. We think she might have left the country...either that or the people she owed money to caught up with her." Nik shrugged, then turned to Nans. "The paper you overheard Corinne talking about was actually just a paper from her bank offering an agreement to avoid the foreclosure. Of course, now she won't have to worry about that."

Nans laughed. "Oh, it sounded so sinister on the phone in light of everything that was going on."

"By the way, I'm curious to know more about your surveillance skills and how you and the Ladies Detective Club investigate things. Can I call you when you get back to Brooke Ridge Falls and pick your brain about a few things?" Nik asked.

Lexy saw a flush creep into Nans' cheeks; her green eyes sparkled. "Well, of course, dear. We're glad to be of help at any time." Nans pulled a business card out of her pocket and handed it to Nik.

"You have business cards?" Lexy's eyes narrowed as she craned to see the card.

"We just had them made," Nans said. She reached back into her pocket to show one to Lexy.

Lexy read it out loud. "Brooke Ridge Falls Ladies Detective Club - We Always Get Our Man." Everyone chuckled and the blush on Nans' cheeks deepened.

"Well, it's been quite a trip," Cassie said.

"Yes, it has. The contest was fun, but I'll be glad to get back home and back to our regular routine," Lexy said.

"Do be sure to say hello to Jack for me," Nik said over the rim of her martini glass.

Lexy nodded, thinking she just might conveniently forget about that.

Cassie checked her watch. "We only have about 40 more minutes before the limo comes to get us...drink up!"

Everyone raised their glasses to their lips, the sound of ice cubes clinking against each other as they drained their drinks was interrupted by a cacophony of bells coming from Nan's gigantic purse.

"What's that?" Nik asked.

"Oh, it's my iPad. One of the girls must be FaceTtiming me." Nans reached down into her purse and pulled out the large tablet. Setting it on the table, she moved the slider with her finger. Ida's face appeared on the screen.

"Hi," Ida said. "Oh, where are you. It looks like you're in a bar!"

"We're all checked out and waiting for our ride to the airport," Nans said.

"Oh, good. You'll be home tonight, then?"

"Yes, how are things there?" Nans asked.

"That's why I'm calling, Mona. Things aren't so good."

Lexy felt a stab of panic. She hoped the ladies were all okay.

"Is everyone all right?" Nans voiced her concern into the iPad.

"Oh, Ruth, Helen, and I are fine. It's not us. Bertram Glumm was found dead in his bed this morning."

Everyone at the table exchanged worried glances.

Nans' hands flew up to her face. "Oh, dear, Bertram seemed so young and spry."

"He was. That's why we need you to come back right away." Ida's face grew larger on the iPad screen, her voice lowered to a whisper. "They're saying it was natural causes, but I think we need to investigate. The girls and I...we have reason to believe he was murdered."

The End.

A Note From The Author

Thanks so much for buying my book! I hope you enjoyed reading it as much as I enjoyed writing it. I would love to hear your feedback and chat with you either through my website or Facebook Fanpage (below). I'm going to be running some great contests and give-aways this year so please do check me out online and join in! Also, if you can find the time to leave a short review of the book on Amazon, it would be much appreciated!

You also might want to check out the other books in the series:

Killer Cupcakes (Lexy Baker Bakery Series Book 1) - Things are going great for Lexy Baker. She's finally opened her dream bakery, gotten rid of her cheating boyfriend and settled into her grandmothers house with her perky dog Sprinkles at her side.

But her blissful life doesn't last long. When her ex boyfriend is found poisoned with cupcakes from her bakery, Lexy finds herself in the middle of a murder investigation headed up by her hunky neighbor detective Jack Perillo.

With the help of a gang of iPad toting, would-be detective grandmothers, Lexy decides to take it upon herself to find the real murderer in order to clear her name and get her bakery back in business.

As things heat up on the murder trail, in the kitchen and between Lexy and the hunky detective, it's a race against time to put the real murderer behind bars and get back to baking.

Will Lexy get her man?

***

Dying For Danish (Lexy Baker Bakery Series Book 2) - When Lexy Baker lands a high paying catering job that allows her to buy some much needed kitchen equipment, she's excited that things are going so well ... until she stumbles over the body of the bride-to-be.

Suddenly Lexy finds herself in a race against time to find the killer. Aided by four iPad toting amateur detective grandma's, her best friend and her little dog Sprinkles, Lexy finds the suspect list growing at every turn.

To make matters worse, the investigation is headed up by her hunky neighbor Detective Jack Perillo who she had been hot and heavy with -

until he mysteriously stopped calling her several weeks earlier.

Add a handsome, rich bachelor who is also a suspect and seems to have designs on Lexy to the mix, and Lexy soon finds that things are not what they seem.

Will Lexy be able to catch the killer in time, or will she end up Dying for Danish?

***

If you like romance, then check out my website for Novellas like:

Reluctant Romance - Risa Kennedy will stop at nothing to save her company. Connor Dunn is a ruthless corporate executive who only cares about the profits. When the two are pitted against each other in a corporate buy out, sparks fly... and not just sparks of anger.

Connor has everything most women find attractive: he's wealthy, astonishingly handsome, successful, charming and he loves his dog Picasso.

But the last thing Risa wants is to be attracted to Connor, especially since he's trying to buy her pet-food company and shut down the low-cost vet clinic that she loves so dearly.

As their worlds collide a spark of attraction turns into a burning desire. But both of them are hiding secrets that could jeopardize everything.

Will Risa and Connor satisfy their desire or will the secrets between them extinguish their reluctant romance?

***

I love to connect with my fans online. You can visit my website to find out about my latest releases here:

http://www.leighanndobbs.com

And if you want to talk to me, head on over to my fanpage on Facebook:
http://www.facebook.com/leighanndobbsbooks

Or, follow me on Twitter:
http://twitter.com/leighanndobbs

About Me:

Leighann Dobbs lives in New Hampshire with her husband and her trusty Chihuahua mix Mojo and beautiful rescue cat, Kitty. She likes to write romance and mystery short stories and novelettes perfect for the busy person on the go. These stories are great for someone who doesn't have a lot of time for reading a full novel. Why not pick one up and escape to another time and place the next time you are waiting for an appointment, enjoying a bath or waiting to pick up the kids at soccer?